Norse Fairy & Folk Tales

Norse Fairy & Folk Tales

SIRIUS

SIRIUS
This edition published in 2019 by Sirius Publishing, a division of Arcturus Publishing Limited,
26/27 Bickels Yard, 151–153 Bermondsey Street,
London SE1 3HA

ISBN: 978-1-78950-399-9
AD007189UK

Printed in China

CONTENTS

INTRODUCTION

In this volume tales come from the collections of three different authors who were well known for their translations of folklore.

George Webbe Dasent was a translator and author born to the attorney General John Roche Dasent and his wife Charlotte Martha in St Vincent in the Caribbean, in 1817. He was well educated and eventually earned a degree in Classical Literature from Oxford University. After his studies, he was appointed to act as secretary to the diplomat Thomas Cartwright in Stockholm, Sweden. It was here that he met Jacob Grimm. At Grimm's recommendation Dasent began to study Scandinavian literature and mythology, and before he returned to England, he had translated and published *The Prose or Younger Edda* and *Grammar of the Icelandic or Old-Norse Tongue*.

After his return, Dasent translated *Popular Tales from the Norse* or *Norske Folkeeventyr*, a collection of folklore that had been gathered by Peter Christen Asbjørnsen and Jørgen Moe, who had, by coincidence, also been inspired by the Brothers Grimm. Using the Grimms' methods of collecting such stories, as well as agreeing with their belief that it was of national import to preserve such things, they set out to do the same for the newly independent Norway. Dasent's stories included here are from this work, first published in 1859.

Charles John Tibbits, born in 1861, was a journalist and newspaper editor and the author of many books of folk tales and legends from a breadth of traditions. He studied at Oxford University and was married to the novelist Annie Olive Brazier. In the prefatory note to his *Folklore and Legends – Scandinavian*, he wrote of Scandinavian folklore, 'Its treasures are many, and of much value. One may be almost sorry to find among them the originals of many of our English tales. Are we indebted to the folk of other nations for all our folk-tales? It would almost seem so.' In one of his tales, 'The Origin of Tiis Lake', a troll is forced to flee town due to the incessant ringing of church bells. This is a common motif used across Scandinavian folklore to explain the absence of trolls.

Katharine Pyle was an American children's author and illustrator who was born in Delaware in 1863. The fourth child of an old Quaker family, she was raised in a household of learning and creativity. Of Katharine, her niece said, 'She was a champion of the underdog and immediately responsive to anyone in need, not always wisely and often at her own expense. Like most crusaders, she had her difficulties and she was constantly challenging both friend and foe but she was a brilliant and vital individual and a woman well ahead of her time.' This brilliance and vitality can be found throughout her work, of which there is much. During her career she produced work prolifically whether writing and illustrating, or editing, which meant that during the years between 1898 and 1934 she produced more than one book a year. *Wonder Tales from Many Lands*, *Three Little Kittens* and *Lazy Matilda, And Other Tales* are just some of the works she produced in this period.

Here are but a few of the many fascinating tales gathered and recorded by all three.

TRUE AND UNTRUE

BY G. W. DASENT

Once on a time, there were two brothers; one was called True, and the other Untrue. True was always upright and good towards all, but Untrue was bad and full of lies, so that no one could believe what he said. Their mother was a widow, and hadn't much to live on; so when her sons had grown up, she was forced to send them away, that they might earn their bread in the world. Each got a little scrip with some food in it, and then they went their way.

Now, when they had walked till evening, they sat down on a windfall in the wood, and took out their scraps, for they were hungry after walking the whole day, and thought a morsel of food would be sweet enough.

'If you're of my mind,' said Untrue, 'I think we had better eat out of your scrip, so long as there is anything in it, and after that we can take to mine.'

Yes, True was well pleased with this, so they fell to eating, but Untrue got all the best bits, and stuffed himself with them, while True got only the burnt crusts and scraps.

Next morning, they broke their fast off True's food, and they dined off it too, and then there was nothing left in his scrip. So when they had walked till late at night, and were ready to eats again, True wanted to eat out of his brother's scrip, but Untrue said 'No,' the food was his, and he had only enough for himself.

'Nay! But you know you ate out of my scrip so long as there was anything in it,' said True.

'All very fine, I daresay,' answered Untrue; 'but if you are such a fool as to let others eat up your food before your face, you must make the best of it, for now all you have to do is to sit here and starve.'

'Very well!' said True, 'you're Untrue by name and untrue by nature; so you have been, and so you will be all your life long.'

Now when Untrue heard this, he flew into a rage, and rushed at his brother, and plucked out both his eyes. 'Now try if you can see whether folk are untrue or not, you blind buzzard!' he said, and so saying, he ran away and left him.

Poor True! there he went walking along and feeling his way through the thick wood. Blind and alone, he scarce knew which way to turn, when all at once he caught hold of the trunk of a great bushy lime tree, so he thought he would climb up into it, and sit there till the night was over for fear of the wild beasts. 'When the birds begin to sing,' he said to himself, 'then I shall know it is day, and I can try to grope my way farther on.' So he climbed up into the lime tree. After he had sat there a little time, he heard how someone came and began to make a stir and clatter under the tree, and soon after others came; and when they began to greet one another, he found out it was Bruin the bear, Greylegs the wolf, Slyboots the fox, and Longears the hare, who had come to keep St. John's Eve under the tree. So they began to eat and drink, and be merry; and when they had done eating, they fell to gossipping together. At last the fox said: 'Shan't we, each of us, tell a little story while we sit here?' Well! the others had nothing against that. It would be good fun, they said, and the bear began; for you may fancy he was king of the company.

'The king of England,', said Bruin, 'has such bad eyesight, he can scarce see a yard before him; but if he only came to this lime tree in the morning, while the dew is still on the leaves, and took and rubbed his eyes with the dew, he would get back his sight as good as ever.'

'Very true!' said Greylegs. 'The king of England has a deaf and dumb daughter too; but if he only knew what I know, he would soon cure her. Last year she went to the communion. She let a crumb of the bread fall out of her mouth, and a great toad came and swallowed it down; but if they only dug up the chancel floor, they would find the toad sitting right under the altar rails, with the bread still sticking in his throat. If they were to cut the toad open and take and give the bread to the princess, she would be like other folk again as to her speech and hearing.'

'That's all very well,' said the fox; 'but if the king of England knew what I know, he would not be so badly off for water in his palace; for under the great stone in his palace yard is a spring of the clearest water one could wish for, if he only knew to dig for it there.'

'Ah!' said the hare in a small voice, 'the king of England has the finest orchard in the whole land, but it does not bear so much as a crab, for there lies a heavy gold chain in three turns round the orchard. If he got that dug up, there would not be a garden like it for bearing in all his kingdom.'

'Very true, I dare say,' said the fox; 'but now it's getting very late, and we may as well go home.' So they all went away together.

After they were gone, True fell asleep as he sat up in the tree, but when the birds began to sing at dawn, he woke up, and took the dew from the leaves and rubbed his eyes with it, and so got his sight back as good as it was before Untrue plucked his eyes out.

Then he went straight to the king of England's palace, and begged for work, and got it on the spot. So one day the king came out into the palace yard, and when he had walked about a bit, he wanted to drink out of his pump; for you must know the day was hot, and the king very thirsty; but when they poured him out a glass, it was so muddy, and nasty, and foul, that the king got quite vexed.

'I don't think there's ever a man in my whole kingdom who has such bad water in his yard as I, and yet I bring it in pipes from far, over hill and dale,' cried out the king.

'Like enough, your Majesty,' said True, 'but if you would let me have some men to help me to dig up this great stone which lies here in the middle of your yard, you would soon see good water, and plenty of it.'

Well, the king was willing enough, and they had scarcely got the stone out, and dug under it a while, before a jet of water sprang out high up into the air, as clear and full as if it came out of a conduit, and clearer water was not to be found in all England.

A little while after the king was out in his palace yard again, and there came a great hawk flying after his chicken, and all the king's men began to clap their hands and bawl out, 'There he flies!' 'There he flies!' The king caught up his gun and tried to shoot the hawk, but he couldn't see so far, so he fell into great grief.

'Would to Heaven,' he said, 'there was anyone who could tell me a cure for my eyes; for I think I shall soon go quite blind!'

'I can tell you one soon enough,' said True. And then he told the king what he had done to cure his own eyes, and the king set off that very afternoon to the lime tree, as you may fancy, and his eyes were quite cured as soon as he rubbed them with the dew which was on the leaves in the morning. From that time forth there was no one whom the king held so dear as True, and he had to be with him wherever he went, both at home and abroad.

So one day, as they were walking together in the orchard, the king said, 'I can't tell how it is *that* I can't! There isn't a man in England who spends so much on his orchard as I, and yet I can't get one of the trees to bear so much as a crab.'

'Well! well!' said True. 'If I may have what lies three times twisted round your orchard, and men to dig it up, your orchard will bear well enough.'

Yes, the king was quite willing, so True got men and began to dig, and at last he dug up the whole gold chain. Now True was a rich man; far richer indeed than the king himself, but still the king was well pleased, for his orchard bore so that the boughs of the trees hung down to the ground, and such sweet apples and pears nobody had ever tasted.

Another day, too, the king and True were walking about, and talking together, when the princess passed them, and the king was quite downcast when he saw her. 'Isn't it a pity, now, that so lovely a princess as mine should want speech and hearing,' he said to True.

'Ay, but there is a cure for that,' said True.

When the king heard that, he was so glad that he promised him the princess to wife, and half his kingdom into the bargain, if he could get her right again. So True took a few men, and went into the church, and dug up the toad which sat under the altar rails. Then he cut open the toad, and took out the bread and gave it to the king's daughter. And from that hour she got back her speech, and could talk like other people.

Now True was to have the princess, and they got ready for the bridal feast, and such a feast had never been seen before; it was the talk of the whole land. Just as they were in the midst of dancing the bridal-dance in came a beggar lad, and begged for a morsel of food, and he was so ragged and wretched that everyone crossed themselves when they looked at him; but True knew him at once, and saw that it was Untrue, his brother.

'Do you know me again?' asked True.

'Oh, where should such a one as I ever have seen so great a lord,' said Untrue.

'Still, you *have* seen me before,' said True. 'It was I whose eyes you plucked out a year ago this very day. Untrue by name, and untrue by nature; so I said before, and so I say now; but you are still my brother, and so you shall have some food. After that, you may go to the lime tree where I sat last year; if you hear anything that can do you good, you will be lucky.'

So Untrue did not wait to be told twice. 'If True has got so much good by sitting in the lime tree, that in one year he has come to be king over half England, what good may not I get,' he wondered. So he set off and climbed up into the lime tree. He had not sat there long before all the beasts came as before, and ate and drank, and kept St. John's Eve under the tree. When they had left off eating, the fox wished that they should begin to tell stories, and Untrue got ready to listen with all his might, till his ears were almost fit to fall off. But Bruin the bear was surly, and growled and said:

'Someone has been chattering about what we said last year, and so now we will hold our tongues about what we know'; and with that the beasts bade one another 'Goodnight', and parted, and Untrue was just as wise as he was before, and the reason was, that his name was Untrue, and his nature untrue too.

EAST O' THE SUN AND WEST O' THE MOON

BY G. W. DASENT

Once on a time, there was a poor husbandman who had so many children that he hadn't much of either food or clothing to give them. Pretty children they all were, but the prettiest was the youngest daughter, who was so lovely there was no end to her loveliness.

So one day – 'twas on a Thursday evening late at the fall of the year – the weather was so wild and rough outside, and it was so cruelly dark, and rain fell and wind blew, till the walls of the cottage shook again. There they all sat round the fire busy with this thing and that. But just then, all at once, something gave three taps on the windowpane. Then the father went out to see what was the matter; and, when he got out of doors, what should he see but a great big white bear.

'Good evening to you!' said the white bear.

'The same to you,' said the man.

'Will you give me your youngest daughter? If you will, I'll make you as rich as you are now poor,' said the bear.

Well, the man would not be at all sorry to be so rich; but still he thought he must have a bit of a talk with his daughter first; so he went in and told them how there was a great white bear waiting outside, who had given his word to make them so rich if he could only have the youngest daughter.

The lassie said 'No!' outright. Nothing could get her to say anything else; so the man went out and settled it with the white bear that he should come again the next Thursday evening and get an answer. Meantime he talked his daughter over, and kept on telling her of all the riches they would get, and how well off she would be herself; and so at last she thought better of it, and washed and mended her rags, made herself as smart as she could, and was ready to start. I can't say her packing gave her much trouble.

Next Thursday evening came the white bear to fetch her, and she got upon his back with her bundle, and off they went. So, when they had gone a bit of the way, the white bear said: 'Are you afraid?'

'No!' she wasn't.

'Well! mind and hold tight by my shaggy coat, and then there's nothing to fear,' said the bear.

So she rode a long, long way, till they came to a great steep hill. There, on the face of it, the white bear gave a knock, and a door opened, and they came into a castle where there were many rooms all lit up; rooms gleaming with silver and gold; and there, too, was a table ready laid, and it was all as grand as grand could be. Then the white bear gave her a silver bell; and when she wanted anything, she was only to ring it, and she would get it at once.

Well, after she had eaten and drunk, and evening wore on, she got sleepy after her journey, and thought she would like to go to bed, so she rang the bell; and she had scarce taken hold of it before she came into a chamber where there was a bed made, as fair and white as anyone would wish to sleep in, with silken pillows and curtains, and gold fringe. All that was in the room was gold or silver; but when she had gone to bed, and put out the light, a man came and laid himself alongside her. That was the white bear, who threw off his beast shape at night; but she never saw him, for he always came after she had put out the light, and before the day dawned he was up and off again. So things went on happily for a while, but at last she began to get silent and sorrowful; for there she went about all day alone, and she longed to go home to see her father and mother and brothers and sisters. So one day, when the white bear asked what it was that she lacked, she said it was so dull and lonely there, and how she longed to go home to see her father and mother, and brothers and sisters, and that was why she was so sad and sorrowful, because she couldn't get to them.

'Well, well!' said the bear, 'perhaps there's a cure for all this; but you must promise me one thing, not to talk alone with your mother, but only when the rest are by to hear; for she'll take you by the hand and try to lead you into a room alone to talk; but you must mind and not do that, else you'll bring bad luck on both of us.'

So one Sunday the white bear came and said now they could set off to see her father and mother. Well, off they started, she sitting on his back, and they went far and long. At last they came to a grand house, and there her brothers and sisters were running about out of doors at play, and everything was so pretty, 'twas a joy to see.

'This is where your father and mother live now,' said the white bear; 'but don't forget what I told you, else you'll make us both unlucky.'

'No!' bless her, she'd not forget; and when she had reached the house, the white bear turned right about and left her.

Then when she went in to see her father and mother, there was such joy, there was no end to it. None of them thought they could thank her enough for all she had done for them. Now, they had everything they wished, as good as good could be, and they all wanted to know how she got on where she lived.

Well, she said, it was very good to live where she did; she had all she wished. What she said beside I don't know; but I don't think any of them had the right end of the stick, or that they got much out of her. But in the afternoon, after they had done dinner, all happened as the white bear had said. Her mother wanted to talk with her alone in her bedroom; but she minded what the white bear had said, and wouldn't go upstairs.

'Oh! what we have to talk about, will keep,' she said, and put her mother off. But somehow or other, her mother got round her at last, and she had to tell her the whole story. So she said, how every night, when she had gone to bed, a man came and lay down beside her as soon as she had put out the light, and how she never saw him, because he was always up and away before the morning dawned; and how she went about woeful and sorrowing, for she thought she should so like to see him, and how all day long she walked about there alone, and how dull, and dreary, and lonesome it was.

'My!' said her mother; 'it may well be a troll you slept with! But now I'll teach you a lesson how to set eyes on him. I'll give you a bit of candle, which you can carry home in your bosom; just light that while he is asleep, but take care not to drop the tallow on him.'

Yes! She took the candle and hid it in her bosom, and as night drew on, the white bear came and fetched her away.

But when they had gone a bit of the way, the white bear asked if all hadn't happened as he had said?

Well, she couldn't say it hadn't.

'Now, mind,'

, said he, 'if you have listened to your mother's advice, you have brought bad luck on us both, and then, all that has passed between us will be as nothing.'

'No,' she said, she hadn't listened to her mother's advice.

So when she reached home, and had gone to bed, it was the old story over again. There came a man and lay down beside her; but at dead of night, when she heard he slept, she got up and struck a light, lit the candle, and let the light shine on him, and so she saw that he was the loveliest prince one ever set eyes on, and she fell so deep in love with him on the spot, that she thought she couldn't live if she didn't give him a kiss there and then. And so she did, but as she kissed him, she dropped three hot drops of tallow on his shirt, and he woke up.

'What have you done?' he cried; 'now you have made us both unlucky, for had you held out only this one year, I had been freed. For I have a stepmother who has bewitched me, so that I am a white bear by day, and a man by night. But now all ties are snapped between us; now I must set off from you to her. She lives in a castle which stands east o' the Sun and west o' the Moon, and there, too, is a princess, with a nose three ells long, and she's the wife I must have now.'

She wept and took it ill, but there was no help for it; go he must.

Then she asked if she mightn't go with him?

No, she mightn't.

'Tell me the way, then,' she said, 'and I'll search you out; *that* surely I may get leave to do.'

'Yes, she might do that,' he said; but there was no way to that place. It lay east o' the Sun and west o' the Moon, and thither she'd never find her way.

So next morning, when she woke up, both prince and castle were gone, and then she lay on a little green patch, in the midst of the gloomy thick wood, and by her side lay the same bundle of rags she had brought with her from her old home.

So when she had rubbed the sleep out of her eyes, and wept till she was tired, she set out on her way, and walked many, many days, till she came to a lofty crag. Under it sat an old hag who played with a gold apple which she tossed about. Her the lassie asked if she knew the way to the prince, who lived with his stepmother in the Castle, that lay east o' the Sun and west o' the Moon, and who was to marry the princess with a nose three ells long.

'How did you come to know about him?' asked the old hag; 'but maybe you are the lassie who ought to have had him?'

Yes, she was.

'So, so; it's you, is it?' said the old hag. 'Well, all I know about him is, that he lives in the castle that lies east o' the Sun and west o' the Moon, and thither you'll come, late or never; but still you may have the loan of my horse, and on him you can ride to my next neighbour. Maybe she'll be able to tell you; and when you get there, just give the horse a switch under the left ear, and beg him to be off home; and, stay, this gold apple you may take with you.'

So she got upon the horse, and rode a long, long time, till she came to another crag, under which sat another old hag, with a gold carding comb. Her the lassie asked if she knew the way to the castle that lay east o' the Sun and west o' the Moon, and she answered, like the first old hag, that she knew nothing about it, except it was east o' the Sun and west o' the Moon.

'And thither you'll come, late or never, but you shall have the loan of my horse to my next neighbour; maybe she'll tell you all about it; and when you get there, just switch the horse under the left ear, and beg him to be off home.'

And this old hag gave her the golden carding comb; it might be she'd find some use for it, she said. So the lassie got up on the horse, and rode a far, far way, and a weary time; and so at last she came to another great crag, under which sat another old hag, spinning with a golden spinning wheel. Her, too, she asked if she knew the way to the Prince, and where the castle was that lay east o' the Sun and west o' the Moon. So it was the same thing over again.

'Maybe it's you who ought to have had the prince?' said the old hag.

Yes, it was.

But she, too, didn't know the way any better than the other two. 'East o' the Sun and west o' the Moon it was,' she knew – that was all.

'And thither you'll come, late or never; but I'll lend you my horse, and then I think you'd best ride to the East Wind and ask him; maybe, he knows those parts, and can blow you thither. But when you get to him, you need only give the horse a switch under the left ear, and he'll trot home of himself.'

And so, too, she gave her the gold spinning wheel. 'Maybe you'll find a use for it,' said the old hag.

Then on she rode many, many days, a weary time, before she got to the East Wind's house, but at last she did reach it, and then she asked the East Wind if he could tell her the way to the prince who dwelt east o' the Sun and west o' the Moon. Yes, the East Wind had often heard tell of it, the prince and the castle, but he couldn't tell the way, for he had never blown so far.

'But, if you will, I'll go with you to my brother the West Wind, maybe he knows, for he's much stronger. So, if you will just get on my back, I'll carry you thither.'

Yes, she got on his back, and I should just think they went briskly along.

So when they got there, they went into the West Wind's house, and the East Wind said the lassie he had brought was the one who ought to have had the prince who lived in the castle east o' the Sun and west o' the Moon; and so she had set out to seek him, and how he had come with her, and would be glad to know if the West Wind knew how to get to the castle.

'Nay,' said the West Wind, 'so far I've never blown; but if you will, I'll go with you to our brother the South Wind, for he's much stronger than either of us, and he has flapped his wings far and wide. Maybe he'll tell you. You can get on my back, and I'll carry you to him.'

Yes, she got on his back, and so they travelled to the South Wind, and weren't so very long on the way, I should think.

When they got there, the West Wind asked him if he could tell her the way to the castle that lay east o' the Sun and west o' the Moon, for it was she who ought to have had the prince who lived there.

'You don't say so! That's she, is it?' said the South Wind.

'Well, I have blustered about in most places in my time, but so far have I never blown; but if you will, I'll take you to my brother the North Wind; he is the oldest and strongest of the whole lot of us, and if he don't know where it is, you'll never find anyone in the world to tell you. You can get on my back, and I'll carry you thither.'

Yes! She got on his back, and away he went from his house at a fine rate. And this time, too, she wasn't long on her way.

So when they got to the North Wind's house, he was so wild and cross, cold puffs came from him a long way off.

'BLAST YOU BOTH, WHAT DO YOU WANT?' he roared out to them ever so far off, so that it struck them with an icy shiver.

'Well,' said the South Wind, 'you needn't be so foul-mouthed, for here I am, your brother, the South Wind, and here is the lassie who ought to have had the Prince who dwells in the castle that lies east o' the Sun and west o' the Moon, and now she wants to ask you if you ever were there, and can tell her the way, for she would be so glad to find him again.'

'YES, I KNOW WELL ENOUGH WHERE IT IS,' said the North Wind; 'once in my life I blew an aspen-leaf thither, but I was so tired I couldn't blow a puff for ever so many days after. But if you really wish to go thither, and aren't afraid to come along with me, I'll take you on my back and see if I can blow you thither.'

Yes, with all her heart; she must, and would, get thither if it were possible in any way; and as for fear, however madly he went, she wouldn't be at all afraid.

'Very well, then,' said the North Wind, 'but you must sleep here tonight, for we must have the whole day before us if we're to get thither at all.'

Early next morning the North Wind woke her, and puffed himself up, and blew himself out, and made himself so stout and big, 'twas gruesome to look at him; and so off they went high up through the air, as if they would never stop till they got to the world's end.

Down here below there was such a storm; it threw down long tracts of wood and many houses, and when it swept over the great sea, ships foundered by hundreds.

So they tore on and on – no one can believe how far they went – and all the while they still went over the sea, and the North Wind got more and more weary, and so out of breath he could scarce bring out a puff, and his wings drooped and drooped, till at last he sunk so low that the crests of the waves dashed over his heels.

'Are you afraid?' said the North Wind.

No, she wasn't.

But they weren't very far from land, and the North Wind had still so much strength left in him that he managed to throw her up on the shore under the windows of the castle which lay east o' the Sun and west o' the Moon; but then he was so weak and worn out, he had to stay there and rest many days before he could get home again.

Next morning, the lassie sat down under the castle window, and began to play with the gold apple, and the first person she saw was the Long-nose who was to have the prince.

'What do you want for your gold apple, you lassie?' asked the Long-nose, and threw up the window.

'It's not for sale, for gold or money,' said the lassie.

'If it's not for sale for gold or money, what is it that you will sell it for? You may name your own price,' said the princess.

'Well! if I may get to the prince, who lives here, and be with him tonight, you shall have it,' said the lassie whom the North Wind had brought.

Yes, she might; that could be done. So the princess got the gold apple; but when the lassie came up to the Prince's bedroom at night he was fast asleep; she called him and shook him, and between whiles she wept sore; but despite all she could do, she couldn't wake him up. Next morning, as soon as day broke, came the princess with the long nose, and drove her out again.

So in the daytime she sat down under the castle windows and began to card with her carding comb, and the same thing happened. The princess asked what she wanted for it; and she said it wasn't for sale for gold or money, but if she might get leave to go up to the prince and be with him that night, the princess should have it. But when she went up she found him fast asleep again, and all she called, and all she shook, and wept, and prayed, she couldn't get life into him; and as soon as the first grey peep of day came, then came the princess with the long nose and chased her out again.

So, in the day time, the lassie sat down outside under the castle window, and began to spin with her golden spinning wheel, and that, too, the princess with the long nose wanted to have. So she threw up the window and asked what she wanted for it. The lassie said, as she had said twice before, it wasn't for sale for gold or money; but if she might go up to the prince who was there, and be with him alone that night, she might have it.

Yes, she might do that and welcome. But now you must know there were some Christian folk who had been carried off thither, and as they sat in their room, which was next to the prince, they had heard how a woman had been in there, and wept and prayed, and called to him two nights running, and they told that to the prince.

That evening, when the princess came with her sleeping draught, the prince made as if he drank, but threw it over his shoulder, for he could guess it was a sleeping draught. So, when the lassie came in, she found the prince wide awake; and then she told him the whole story how she had come thither.

'Ah,' said the prince, 'you've just come in the very nick of time, for tomorrow is to be our wedding day; but now I won't have the Long-nose, and you are the only woman in the world who can set me free. I'll say I want to see what my wife is fit for, and beg her to wash the shirt which has the three spots of tallow on it; she'll say yes, for she doesn't know 'tis you who put them there; but that's a work only for Christian folk, and not for such a pack of trolls, and so I'll say that I won't have any other for my bride than the woman who can wash them out, and ask you to do it.'

So there was great joy and love between them all that night. But next day, when the wedding was to be, the prince said:

'First of all, I'd like to see what my bride is fit for.'

'Yes,' said the step-mother, with all her heart.

'Well,' said the prince, 'I've got a fine shirt which I'd like for my wedding shirt, but somehow or other it has got three spots of tallow on it, which I must have washed out; and I have sworn never to take any other bride than the woman who's able to do that. If she can't, she's not worth having.'

Well, that was no great thing they said, so they agreed, and she with the long-nose began to wash away as hard as she could, but the more she rubbed and scrubbed, the bigger the spots grew.

'Ah!' said the old hag, her mother, 'you can't wash; let me try.'

But she hadn't long taken the shirt in hand, before it got far worse than ever, and with all her rubbing, and wringing, and scrubbing, the spots grew bigger and blacker, and the darker and uglier was the shirt.

Then all the other trolls began to wash, but the longer it lasted, the blacker and uglier the shirt grew, till at last it was as black all over as if it had been up the chimney.

'Ah!' said the prince, 'you're none of you worth a straw if you can't wash. Why there, outside, sits a beggar lassie, I'll be bound she knows how to wash better than the whole lot of you. COME IN LASSIE!' he shouted.

Well, in she came.

'Can you wash this shirt clean, lassie, you?' said he.

'I don't know,' she said, 'but I think I can'.

And almost before she had taken it and dipped it in the water, it was as white as driven snow, and whiter still.

'Yes, you are the lassie for me,' said the prince.

At that the old hag flew into such a rage, she burst on the spot, and the Princess with the long nose after her, and the whole pack of trolls after her – at least I've never heard a word about them since.

As for the prince and princess, they set free all the poor Christian folk who had been carried off and shut up there; and they took with them all the silver and gold, and flitted away as far as they could from the castle that lay east o' the Sun and west o' the Moon.

BOOTS WHO HAD AN EATING MATCH WITH A TROLL

BY G. W. DASENT

Once on a time, there was a farmer who had three sons; his means were small, and he was old and weak, and his sons would take to nothing. A fine large wood belonged to the farm, and one day the father told his sons to go and hew wood, and try to pay off some of his debts.

Well, after a long talk he got them to set off, and the eldest was to go first. But when he had got well into the wood, and began to hew at a mossy old fir, what should he see coming up to him but a great sturdy troll.

'If you hew in this wood of mine,' said the troll, 'I'll kill you!'

When the lad heard that, he threw the axe down, and ran off home as fast as he could lay legs to the ground; so he came in quite out of breath, and told them what had happened, but his father called him 'hare-heart' – no troll would ever have scared him from hewing when he was young, he said.

Next day the second son's turn came, and he fared just the same. He had scarce hewn three strokes at the fir, before the troll came to him too, and said:

'If you hew in this wood of mine, I'll kill you.'

The lad dared not so much as look at him, but threw down the axe, took to his heels, and came scampering home just like his brother. So when he got home, his father was angry again, and said no troll had ever scared him when he was young.

The third day Boots wanted to set off.

'You, indeed!' said the two elder brothers; 'you'll do it bravely, no doubt – you, who have scarce ever set your foot out of the door.'

Boots said nothing to this, but only begged them to give him a good store of food. His mother had no cheese, so she set the pot on the fire to make him a little, and he put it into a scrip and set off. So when he had hewn a bit, the troll came to him too, and said:

'If you hew in this wood of mine, I'll kill you.'

But the lad was not slow; he pulled his cheese out of the scrip in a trice, and squeezed it till the whey spurted out.

'Hold your tongue!' he cried to the troll, 'or I'll squeeze you as I squeeze the water out of this white stone.'

'Nay, dear friend!' said the troll, 'only spare me, and I'll help you to hew.'

Well, on those terms the lad was willing to spare him, and the troll hewed so bravely, that they felled and cut up many, many fathoms in the day.

But when evening drew near, the troll said:

'Now you'd better come home with me, for my house is nearer than yours.'

So the lad was willing enough; and when they reached the troll's house, the troll was to make up the fire, while the lad went to fetch water for their porridge, and there stood two iron pails so big and heavy, that he couldn't so much as lift them from the ground.

'Pooh!' said the lad, 'it isn't worthwhile to touch these finer-basins: I'll just go and fetch the spring itself.'

'Nay, nay, dear friend!' said the troll; 'I can't afford to lose my spring; just you make up the fire, and I'll go and fetch the water.'

So when he came back with the water, they set to and boiled up a great pot of porridge.

'It's all the same to me,' said the lad; 'but if you're of my mind, we'll have an eating match!'

'With all my heart,' said the troll, for he thought he could surely hold his own in eating. So they sat down; but the lad took his scrip unbeknownst to the Troll, and hung it before him, and so he spooned more into the scrip than he ate himself; and when the scrip was full, he took up his knife and made a slit in it. The troll looked on all the while, but said never a word. So when they had eaten a good bit longer, the troll laid down his spoon, saying, 'Nay, but I can't eat a morsel more.'

'But you shall eat,' said the youth; 'I'm only half done; why don't you do as I did, and cut a hole in your paunch? You'll be able to eat then as much as you please.'

'But doesn't it hurt one cruelly?' asked the troll.

'Oh,' said the youth, 'nothing to speak of.'

So the troll did as the lad said, and then you must know very well that he lost his life; but the lad took all the silver and gold that he found in the hillside, and went home with it, and you may fancy it went a great way to pay off the debt.

HACON GRIZZLEBEARD

BY G. W. DASENT

Once on a time, there was a princess who was so proud and pert that no suitor was good enough for her. She made a game of them all, and sent them about their business, one after the other; but though she was so proud, still new suitors kept on coming to the palace, for she was a beauty, the wicked hussey!

So one day, there came a prince to woo her, and his name was Hacon Grizzlebeard; but the first night he was there, the princess bade the king's fool cut off the ears of one of the prince's horses, and slit the jaws of the other up to the ears. When the prince went out to drive next day, the princess stood in the porch and looked at him.

'Well!' she cried, 'I never saw the like of this in all my life; the keen north wind that blows here has taken the ears off one of your horses, and the other has stood by and gaped at what was going on till his jaws have split right up to his ears.'

And with that she burst out into a roar of laughter, ran in, slammed to the door, and let him drive off.

So he drove home; but as he went, he thought to himself that he would pay her off one day. After a bit, he put on a great beard of moss, threw a great fur cloak over his clothes, and dressed himself up just like any beggar. He went to a goldsmith and bought a golden spinning wheel, and sat down with it under the princess' window, and began to file away at his spinning wheel, and to turn it this way and that, for it wasn't quite in order, and, besides, it wanted a stand.

So when the princess rose up in the morning, she came to the window and threw it up, and called out to the beggar if he would sell his golden spinning wheel?

'No; it isn't for sale,' said Hacon Grizzlebeard; 'but if I may have leave to sleep outside your bedroom door tonight, I'll give it you.'

Well, the princess thought it a good bargain; there could be no danger in letting him sleep outside her door.

So she got the wheel, and at night Hacon Grizzlebeard lay down outside her bedroom. But as the night wore on he began to freeze. 'Hutetutetutetu! It is *so* cold; do let me in,' he cried.

'You've lost your wits outright, I think,' said the princess.

'Oh, hutetutetutetu! It is so bitter cold, pray do let me in,' said Hacon Grizzlebeard again.

'Hush! hush! Hold your tongue!' said the princess; 'if my father were to know that there was a man in the house, I should be in a fine scrape.'

'Oh, hutetutetutetu! I'm almost frozen to death. Only let me come inside and lie on the floor,' said Hacon Grizzlebeard.

Yes! there was no help for it. She had to let him in, and when he was, he lay on the ground and slept like a top.

Some time after, Hacon came again with the stand to the spinning wheel, and sat down under the princess' window, and began to file at it, for it was not quite fit for use. When she heard him filing, she threw up the window and began to talk to him, and to ask what he had there.

'Oh, only the stand to that spinning wheel which your Royal Highness bought; for I thought, as you had the wheel, you might like to have the stand too.'

'What do you want for it?' asked the princess; but it was not for sale any more than the wheel, although she might have it if she would give him leave to sleep on the floor of her bedroom next night.

Well! she gave him leave, only he was to be sure to lie still, and not to shiver and call out 'hutetu', or any such stuff. Hacon Grizzlebeard promised fair enough, but as the night wore on he began to shiver and shake, and to ask whether he might not come nearer, and lie on the floor alongside the princess' bed.

There was no help for it; she had to give him leave, lest the king should hear the noise he made. So Hacon Grizzlebeard lay alongside the princess' bed, and slept like a top.

It was a long while before Hacon Grizzlebeard came again; but when he came he had with him a golden wool winder, and he sat down and began to file away at it under the princess' window. Then came the old story over again. When the princess heard what was going on, she came to the window, and asked him how he did, and whether he would sell the golden wool winder?

'It is not to be had for money; but if you'll give me leave to sleep tonight in your bedroom, with my head on your bedstead, you shall have it for nothing,' said Hacon Grizzlebeard.

Well! she would give him leave, if he only gave his word to be quiet, and make no noise. So he said he would do his best to be still; but as the night wore on, he began to shiver and shake so, that his teeth chattered again.

'Hutetutetutetu! It is so bitter cold! Oh, do let me get into bed and warm myself a little,' said Hacon Grizzlebeard.

'Get into bed!' said the princess; 'why, you must have lost your wits.'

'Hutetutetutetu!' said Hacon; 'do let me get into bed. Hutetutetutetu.'

'Hush! hush! be still for God's sake,' said the princess; 'if father knows there is a man in here, I shall be in a sad plight. I'm sure he'll kill me on the spot.'

'Hutetutetutetu! let me get into bed,' said Hacon Grizzlebeard, who kept on shivering so that the whole room shook.

Well, there was no help for it; she had to let him get into bed, where he slept both sound and soft; but a little while after the princess had a child, at which the king grew so wild with rage, that he was near making an end of both mother and babe. Just after this happened, came Hacon Grizzlebeard tramping that way once more, as if by chance, and took his seat down in the kitchen, like any other beggar.

So when the princess came out and saw him, she cried, 'Ah, God have mercy on me, for the ill-luck you have brought on me; father is ready to burst with rage; do let me follow you to your home.'

'Oh! I'll be bound you're too well bred to follow me,' said Hacon, 'for I have nothing but a log but to live in; and how I shall ever get food for you I can't tell, for it's just as much as I can do to get food for myself.'

'Oh yes! It's all the same to me how you get it, or whether you get it at all,' she said; 'only let me be with you, for if I stay here any longer, my father will be sure to take my life.'

So she got leave to be with the beggar, as she called him, and they walked a long, long way, though she was but a poor hand at tramping. When she passed out of her father's land into another, she asked whose it was?

'Oh, this is Hacon Grizzlebeard's, if you must know,' said he.

'Indeed!' said the Princess; 'I might have married him if I chose, and then I should not have had to walk about like a beggar's wife.'

So whenever they came to grand castles, and woods, and parks, and she asked whose they were? the beggar's answer was still the same: 'Oh, they are Hacon Grizzlebeard's.' And the princess was in a sad way that she had not chosen the man who had such broad lands. Last of all, they came to a palace, where he said he was known, and where he thought he could get her work, so that they might have something to live on. So he built up a cabin by the woodside for them to dwell in; and every day he went to the king's palace, as he said, to hew wood and draw water for the cook, and when he came back he brought a few scraps of meat; but they did not go very far. One day, when he came home from the palace, he said: 'Tomorrow I will stay at home and look after the baby, but you must get ready to go to the palace, do you hear, for the prince said you were to come and try your hand at baking.'

'I...bake!' exclaimed the princess; 'I can't bake, for I never did such a thing in my life.'

'Well, you must go,' said Hacon, 'since the prince has said it. If you can't bake, you can learn; you have only got to look how the rest bake; and mind, when you leave, you must steal me some bread.'

'I can't steal,' said the princess.

'You can learn that too,' said Hacon. 'You know we live on short commons. But take care that the prince doesn't see you, for he has eyes at the back of his head.'

So when she was well on her way, Hacon ran by a short cut and reached the palace long before her, and threw off his rags and beard, and put on his princely robes.

The princess took her turn in the bakehouse, and did as Hacon bade her, for she stole bread till her pockets were crammed full. So when she was about to go home at even, the prince said: 'We don't know much of this old wife of Hacon Grizzlebeard's, I think we'd best see if she has taken anything away with her.'

So he thrust his hand into all her pockets, and felt her all over, and when he found the bread, he was in a great rage, and led them all a sad life. She began to weep and bewail, and said: 'The beggar made me do it, and I couldn't help it.'

'Well,' said the prince at last, 'it ought to have gone hard with you; but all the same, for the sake of the beggar you shall be forgiven this once.'

When she was well on her way, he threw off his robes, put on his skin cloak, and his false beard, and reached the cabin before her. When she came home, he was busy nursing the baby.

'Well, you have made me do what it went against my heart to do. This is the first time I ever stole, and this shall be the last.' And with that she told him how it had gone with her, and what the prince had said.

A few days after Hacon Grizzlebeard came home at even and said: 'Tomorrow I must stay at home and mind the babe, for they are going to kill a pig at the palace, and you must help to make the sausages.'

'I make sausages!' exclaimed the princess; 'I can't do any such thing. I have eaten sausages often enough, but as to making them, I never made one in my life.'

Well, there was no help for it; the prince had said it, and go she must. As for not knowing how, she was only to do what the others did, and at the same time Hacon bade her steal some sausages for him.

'Nay, but I can't steal them,' she said; 'you know how it went last time.'

'Well, you can learn to steal; who knows but you may have better luck next time,' said Hacon Grizzlebeard.

When she was well on her way, Hacon ran by a short cut, reached the palace long before her, threw off his skin cloak and false beard, and stood in the kitchen with his royal robes before she came in. So the princess stood by when the pig was killed, and made sausages with the rest, and did as Hacon bade her, and stuffed her pockets full of sausages. But when she was about to go home at even, the prince said, 'This beggar's wife was long-fingered last time; we may as well just see if she hasn't carried anything off.'

So he began to thrust his hands into her pockets, and when he found the sausages, he was in a great rage again, and made a great to do, threatening to send for the constable and put her into the cage.

'Oh, God bless your Royal Highness, do let me off! The beggar made me do it,' she said, and wept bitterly.

'Well,' said Hacon, 'you ought to smart for it; but for the beggar's sake you shall be forgiven.'

When she was gone, he changed his clothes again, ran by the short cut, and when she reached the cabin, there he was before her. Then she told him the whole story, and swore, through thick and thin, it should be the last time he got her to do such a thing.

Now, it fell out a little time after, when the man came back from the palace, he said, 'Our prince is going to be married, but the bride is sick, so the tailor can't measure her for her wedding gown. And the prince's will is that you should go up to the palace and be measured instead of the bride; for he says you are just the same height and shape. But after you have been measured, mind you don't go away; you can stand about, you know, and when the tailor cuts out the gown, you can snap up the largest pieces and bring them home for a waistcoat for me.'

'Nay, but I can't steal,' she said. 'Besides, you know how it went last time.'

'You can learn then,' said Hacon, 'and you may have better luck, perhaps.'

She thought it bad, but still she went and did as she was told. She stood by while the tailor was cutting out the gown, and she swept down all the biggest scraps, and stuffed them into her pockets; and when she was going away, the prince said, 'We may as well see if this old girl has not been long-fingered this time too.'

So he began to feel and search her pockets, and when he found the pieces he was in a rage, and began to stamp and scold at a great rate, while she wept and said, 'Ah, pray forgive me; the beggar bade me do it, and I couldn't help it.'

'Well, you ought to smart for it,' said Hacon; 'but for the beggar's sake it shall be forgiven you.'

So it went now just as it had gone before, and when she got back to the cabin, the beggar was there before her.

'Oh, Heaven help me,' she said. 'You will be the death of me at last, by making me nothing but what is wicked. The prince was in such a towering rage that he threatened me both with the constable and the cage.'

Sometime after, Hacon came home to the cabin at even and said, 'Now, the prince's will is, that you should go up to the palace and stand for the bride, old lass, for the bride is still sick, and keeps her bed. But he won't put off the wedding, and he says, you are so like her, that no one could tell one from the other. So tomorrow you must get ready to go to the palace.'

'I think you've lost your wits, both the prince and you,' said she. 'Do you think I look fit to stand in the bride's place? look at me! Can any beggar's trull look worse than I?'

'Well, the prince said you were to go, and so go you must,' said Hacon Grizzlebeard.

There was no help for it, go she must; and when she reached the palace, they dressed her out so finely that no princess ever looked so smart.

The bridal train went to church, where she stood for the bride, and when they came back, there was dancing and merriment in the palace. But just as she was in the midst of dancing with the prince, she saw a gleam of light through the window, and lo, the cabin by the wood was all one bright flame.

'Oh! The beggar, and the babe, and the cabin,' she screamed out, and was just going to swoon away.

'Here is the beggar, and there is the babe, and so let the cabin burn away,' said Hacon Grizzlebeard.

Then she knew him again, and after that the mirth and merriment began in right earnest; but since that I have never heard tell anything more about them.

THE GIANT WHO HAD NO HEART IN HIS BODY

BY G. W. DASENT

Once on a time, there was a king who had seven sons, and he loved them so much that he could never bear to be without them all at once, but one must always be with him. Now, when they were grown up, six were to set off to woo, but as for the youngest, his father kept him at home, and the others were to bring back a princess for him to the palace. So the king gave the six the finest clothes you ever set eyes on, so fine that the light gleamed from them a long way off, and each had his horse, which cost many, many hundred dollars, and so they set off. Now, when they had been to many palaces, and seen many princesses, at last they came to a king who had six daughters; such lovely king's daughters they had never seen, and so they fell to wooing them, each one, and when they had got them for sweethearts, they set off home again, but they quite forgot that they were to bring back with them a sweetheart for Boots, their brother, who stayed at home, for they were over head and ears in love with their own sweethearts.

But when they had gone a good bit on their way, they passed close by a steep hillside, like a wall, where the giant's house was, and there the giant came out, and set his eyes upon them, and turned them all into stone, princes and princesses and all. Now the king waited and waited for his six sons, but the more he waited, the longer they stayed away. So he fell into great trouble, and said he should never know what it was to be glad again.

'And if I had not you left,' he said to Boots, 'I would live no longer, so full of sorrow am I for the loss of your brothers.'

'Well, but now I've been thinking to ask your leave to set out and find them again; that's what I'm thinking of', said Boots.

'Nay, nay!' said his father, 'that leave you shall never get, for then you would stay away too.'

But Boots had set his heart upon it; go he would; and he begged and prayed so long that the king was forced to let him go. Now, you must know the king had no other horse to give Boots but an old broken-down jade, for his six other sons and their train had carried off all his horses; but Boots did not care a pin for that – he sprang up on his sorry-old steed.

'Farewell, father,' said he. 'I'll come back, never fear, and like enough I shall bring my six brothers back with me.' And with that, he rode off.

So, when he had ridden a while, he came to a raven, which lay in the road and flapped its wings, and was not able to get out of the way, it was so starved.

'Oh, dear friend,' said the raven, 'give me a little food, and I'll help you again at your utmost need.'

'I haven't much food,' said the prince, 'and I don't see how you'll ever be able to help me much; but still I can spare you a little. I see you want it.'

So he gave the raven some of the food he had brought with him.

Now, when he had gone a bit further, he came to a brook, and in the brook lay a great salmon, which had got upon a dry place and dashed itself about, and could not get into the water again.

'Oh, dear friend,' said the salmon to the prince; 'shove me out into the water again, and I'll help you again at your utmost need.'

'Well!' said the prince, 'the help you'll give me will not be great, I daresay, but it's a pity you should lie there and choke.' And with that he shot the fish out into the stream again.

After that, he went a long, long way, and there met him a wolf, which was so famished that it lay and crawled along the road on its belly.

'Dear friend, do let me have your horse,' said the Wolf. 'I'm so hungry the wind whistles through my ribs; I've had nothing to eat these two years.'

'No,' said Boots, 'this will never do. First I came to a raven, and I was forced to give him my food; next I came to a salmon, and him I had to help into the water again; and now you will have my horse. It can't be done, that it can't, for then I should have nothing to ride on.'

'Nay, dear friend, but you can help me,' said Graylegs the wolf. 'You can ride upon my back, and I'll help you again in your utmost need.'

'Well, the help I shall get from you will not be great, I'll be bound,' said the prince; 'but you may take my horse, since you are in such need.'

So when the wolf had eaten the horse, Boots took the bit and put it into the wolf's jaw, and laid the saddle on his back; and now the wolf was so strong, after what he had got inside, that he set off with the prince like nothing. So fast he had never ridden before.

'When we have gone a bit farther,' said Graylegs, 'I'll show you the giant's house.'

So after a while they came to it.

'See, here is the giant's house,' said the wolf. 'And see, here are your six brothers, whom the giant has turned into stone; and see here are their six brides, and away yonder is the door, and in at that door you must go.'

'Nay, but I daren't go in,' said the prince; 'he'll take my life.'

'No! no!' said the Wolf; 'when you get in you'll find a princess, and she'll tell you what to do to make an end of the giant. Only mind and do as she bids you.'

Well! Boots went in, but, truth to say, he was very much afraid. When he came in the giant was away, but in one of the rooms sat the princess, just as the wolf had said, and so lovely a princess Boots had never yet set eyes on.

'Oh, heaven help you! Whence have you come?' exclaimed the princess, when she saw him. 'It will surely be your death. No one can make an end of the giant who lives here, for he has no heart in his body.'

'Well! well!' said Boots. 'But now that I am here, I may as well try what I can do with him; and I will see if I can't free my brothers, who are standing turned to stone out of doors; and you, too, I will try to save, that I will.'

'Well, if you must, you must,' said the princess; 'and so let us see if we can't hit on a plan. Just creep under the bed yonder, and mind and listen to what he and I talk about. But, pray, do lie as still as a mouse.'

So he crept under the bed, and he had scarce got well underneath it, before the giant came.

'Ha!' roared the giant, 'what a smell of Christian blood there is in the house!'

'Yes, I know there is,' said the princess, 'for there came a magpie flying with a man's bone, and let it fall down the chimney.

I made all the haste I could to get it out, but all one can do, the smell doesn't go off so soon.'

So the giant said no more about it, and when night came, they went to bed. After they had lain awhile, the princess said:

'There is one thing I'd be so glad to ask you about, if I only dared.'

'What thing is that?' asked the giant.

'Only where it is you keep your heart, since you don't carry it about you,' said the princess.

'Ah! that's a thing you've no business to ask about; but if you must know, it lies under the door-sill,' said the giant.

'Ho! ho!' said Boots to himself under the bed, 'then we'll soon see if we can't find it.'

Next morning, the giant got up cruelly early, and strode off to the wood; but he was hardly out of the house before Boots and the princess set to work to look under the door-sill for his heart; but the more they dug, and the more they hunted, the more they couldn't find it.

'He has baulked us this time,' said the princess, 'but we'll try him once more.'

So she picked all the prettiest flowers she could find, and strewed them over the door-sill, which they had laid in its right place again; and when the time came for the giant to come home again, Boots crept under the bed. Just as he was well under, back came the giant.

Snuff, snuff, went the giant's nose. 'My eyes and limbs, what a smell of Christian blood there is in here,' said he.

'I know there is,' said the princess, 'for there came a magpie flying with a man's bone in his bill, and let it fall down the chimney. I made as much haste as I could to get it out, but I daresay it's that you smell.'

So the giant held his peace, and said no more about it. A little while after, he asked who it was that had strewed flowers about the door-sill.

'Oh, I, of course,' said the princess.

'And, pray, what's the meaning of all this?' asked the giant.

'Ah!' said the princess, 'I'm so fond of you that I couldn't help strewing them, when I knew that your heart lay under there.'

'You don't say so,' said the giant, 'but after all it doesn't lie there at all.'

So when they went to bed again in the evening, the princess asked the giant again where his heart was, for she said she would so like to know.

'Well,' said the giant, 'if you must know, it lies away yonder in the cupboard against the wall.'

'So, so!' thought Boots and the princess, 'then we'll soon try to find it.'

Next morning the giant was away early, and strode off to the wood, and so soon as he was gone Boots and the princess were in the cupboard hunting for his heart, but the more they sought for it, the less they found it.

'Well,' said the princess, 'we'll just try him once more.'

So she decked out the cupboard with flowers and garlands, and when the time came for the giant to come home, Boots crept under the bed again.

Then back came the giant.

Snuff, snuff! 'My eyes and limbs, what a smell of Christian blood there is in here!'

'I know there is,' said the princess, 'for a little while since there came a magpie flying with a man's bone in his bill, and let it fall down the chimney. I made all the haste I could to get it out of the house again, but after all my pains, I daresay it's that you smell.'

When the giant heard that, he said no more about it, but a little while after, he saw how the cupboard was all decked about with flowers and garlands, so he asked who it was that had done that? Who could it be but the princess.

'And, pray, what's the meaning of all this tomfoolery?' asked the giant.

'Oh, I'm so fond of you, I couldn't help doing it when I knew that your heart lay there,' said the princess.

'How can you be so silly as to believe any such thing?' asked the giant.

'Oh yes, how can I help believing it, when you say it?' said the princess.

'You're a goose,' said the giant. 'Where my heart is, you will never come.'

'Well,' said the princess;' but for all that, 'twould be such a pleasure to know where it really lies.'

Then the poor giant could hold out no longer, but was forced to say: 'Far, far away in a lake lies an island; on that island stands a church; in that church is a well; in that well swims a duck; in that duck there is an egg, and in that egg there lies my heart – you darling!'

In the morning early, while it was still grey dawn, the giant strode off to the wood.

'Yes! now I must set off too,' said Boots. 'If I only knew how to find the way.' He took a long, long farewell of the princess, and when he got out of the giant's door, there stood the wolf waiting for him. So Boots told him all that had happened inside the house, and said now he wished to ride to the well in the church, if he only knew the way. So the wolf bade him jump on his back, he'd soon find the way; and away they went, till the wind whistled after them, over hedge and field, over hill and dale. After they had travelled many, many days, they came at last to the lake. Then the prince did not know how to get over it, but the wolf bade him only not be afraid, but stick on, and so he jumped into the lake with the prince on his back, and swam over to the island. So they came to the church; but the church keys hung high, high up on the top of the tower, and at first the prince did not know how to get them down.

'You must call on the raven,' said the wolf.

So the prince called on the raven, and in a trice the raven came, and flew up and fetched the keys, and so the prince got into the church. But when he came to the well, there lay the duck, and swam about backwards and forwards, just as the giant had said. So the prince stood and coaxed it and coaxed it, till it came to him, and he grasped it in his hand; but just as he lifted it up from the water the duck dropped the egg into the well, and then Boots was beside himself to know how to get it out again.

'Well, now you must call on the salmon to be sure,' said the wolf; and the king's son called on the salmon, and the salmon came and fetched up the egg from the bottom of the well.

Then the wolf told him to squeeze the egg, and as soon as ever he squeezed it the giant screamed out.

'Squeeze it again,' said the wolf; and when the prince did so, the giant screamed still more piteously, and begged and prayed so prettily to be spared, saying he would do all that the prince wished if he would only not squeeze his heart in two.

'Tell him, if he will restore to life again your six brothers and their brides, whom he has turned to stone, you will spare his life,' said the wolf. Yes, the giant was ready to do that, and he turned the six brothers into king's sons again, and their brides into king's daughters.

'Now, squeeze the egg in two,' said the wolf. So Boots squeezed the egg to pieces, and the giant burst at once.

Now, when he had made an end of the giant, Boots rode back again on the wolf to the giant's house, and there stood all his six brothers alive and merry, with their brides. Then Boots went into the hillside after his bride, and so they all set off home again to their father's house. And you may fancy how glad the old king was when he saw all his seven sons come back, each with his bride. 'But the loveliest bride of all is the bride of Boots, after all,' said the king, 'and he shall sit uppermost at the table, with her by his side.'

So he sent out, and called a great wedding feast, and the mirth was both loud and long, and if they have not done feasting, why, they are still at it.

THE MASTERMAID

BY G. W. DASENT

Once on a time, there was a king who had several sons – I don't know how many there were – but the youngest had no rest at home, for nothing else would please him but to go out into the world and try his luck, and after a long time the king was forced to give him leave to go. Now, after he had travelled some days, he came one night to a giant's house, and there he got a place in the giant's service. In the morning the giant went off to herd his goats, and as he left the yard, he told the prince to clean out the stable; 'and after you have done that, you needn't do anything else today; for you must know it is an easy master you have come to. But what is set you to do you must do well, and you mustn't think of going into any of the rooms which are beyond that in which you slept, for if you do, I'll take your life.'

'Sure enough, it is an easy master I have got,' said the prince to himself as he walked up and down the room, and carolled and sang, for he thought there was plenty of time to clean out the stable. 'But still it would be good fun just to peep into his other rooms, for there must be something in them which he is afraid lest I should see, since he won't give me leave to go in.'

So he went into the first room, and there was a pot boiling on a hook by the wall, but the prince saw no fire underneath it. I wonder what is inside it, he thought; and then he dipped a lock of his hair into it, and the hair seemed as if it were all turned to copper.

'What a dainty broth,' he said; 'if one tasted it, he'd look grand inside his gullet.' And with that he went into the next room. There, too, was a pot hanging by a hook, which bubbled and boiled, but there was no fire under that either.

'I may as well try this too,' said the prince, as he put another lock into the pot, and it came out all silvered.

'They haven't such rich broth in my father's house,' said the prince; 'but it all depends on how it tastes,' and with that he went on into the third room. There, too, hung a pot, and boiled just as he had seen in the two other rooms, and the prince had a mind to try this too, so he dipped a lock of hair into it, and it came out gilded, so that the light gleamed from it.

'"Worse and worse", said the old wife; but I say better and better,' said the prince; 'but if he boils gold here, I wonder what he boils in yonder.'

He thought he might as well see, so he went through the door into the fourth room. Well, there was no pot in there, but there was a princess, seated on a bench, so lovely, that the prince had never seen anything like her in his born days.

'Oh! in Heaven's name,' she said, 'what do you want here?'

'I got a place here yesterday', said the prince.

'A place, indeed! Heaven help you out of it.'

'Well, after all, I think I've got an easy master; he hasn't set me much to do today, for after I have cleaned out the stable, my day's work is over.'

'Yes, but how will you do it,' she asked, 'for if you set to work to clean it like other folk, ten pitchforks full will come in for everyone you toss out. But I will teach you how to set to work: you must turn the fork upside down, and toss with the handle, and then all the dung will fly out of itself.'

Yes, he would be sure to do that, said the prince; and so he sat there the whole day, for he and the princess were soon great friends, and had made up their minds to have one another, and so the first day of his service with the giant was not long, you may fancy. But when the evening drew on, she said 'twould be as well if he got the stable cleaned out before the giant came home; and when he went to the stable, he thought he would just see if what she had said were true, and so he began to work like the grooms in his father's stable; but he soon had enough of that, for he hadn't worked a minute before the stable was so full of dung that he hadn't room to stand. Then he did as the princess bade him, and turned up the fork and worked with the handle, and lo, in a trice the stable was as clean as if it had been scoured. And when he had done his work, he went back into the room where the giant had given him leave to be, and began to walk up and down, and to carol and sing. So after a bit, home came the giant with his goats.

'Have you cleaned the stable?' asked the giant.

'Yes, now it's all right and tight, master,' answered the prince.

'I'll soon see if it is,' growled the giant, and strode off to the stable, where he found it just as the prince had said.

'You've been talking to my Mastermaid, I can see,' said the giant; 'for you've not sucked this knowledge out of your own breast.'

'Mastermaid!' said the prince, who looked as stupid as an owl, 'what sort of thing is that, master? I'd be very glad to see it.'

'Well, well!' said the giant; 'you'll see her soon enough.'

Next day, the giant set off with his goats again, and before he went he told the prince to fetch home his horse, which was out at grass on the hillside, and when he had done that he might rest all the day.

'For you must know, it is an easy master you have come to,' said the giant; 'but if you go into any of the rooms I spoke of yesterday, I'll wring your head off.'

So off he went with his flock of goats.

'An easy master you are indeed,' said the prince, 'but for all that, I'll just go in and have a chat with your Mastermaid – maybe she'll be as soon mine as yours.' So he went in to her, and she asked him what he had to do that day.

'Oh, nothing to be afraid of,' said he; 'I've only to go up to the hillside to fetch his horse.'

'Very well, and how will you set about it?'

'Well, for that matter, there's no great art in riding a horse home. I fancy I've ridden fresher horses before now,' said the prince.

'Ah, but this isn't so easy a task as you think; but I'll teach you how to do it. When you get near it, fire and flame will come out of its nostrils, as out of a tar barrel; but look out, and take the bit which hangs behind the door yonder, and throw it right into his jaws, and he will grow so tame that you may do what you like with him.'

Yes, the prince would mind and do that; and so he sat in there the whole day, talking and chattering with the Mastermaid about one thing and another, but they always came back to how happy they would be if they could only have one another, and get well away from the giant; and, to tell the truth, the prince would have clean forgotten both the horse and the hillside, if the Mastermaid hadn't put him in mind of them when evening drew on, telling him he had better set out to fetch the horse before the giant came home. So he set off, and took the bit which hung in the corner, ran up the hill, and it wasn't long before he met the horse, with fire and flame streaming out of its nostrils. But he watched his time, and, as the horse came open-jawed up to him, he threw the bit into its mouth, and it stood as quiet as a lamb. After that, it was no great matter to ride it home and put it up, you may fancy; and then the prince went into his room again, and began to carol and sing.

So the giant came home again at even with his goats; and the first words he said were: 'Have you brought my horse down from the hill?'

'Yes, master, that I have,' said the prince; 'and a better horse I never bestrode; but for all that I rode him straight home, and put him up safe and sound.'

'I'll soon see to that,' said the giant, and ran out to the stable, and there stood the horse just as the prince had said.

'You've talked to my Mastermaid, I'll be bound, for you haven't sucked this out of your own breast,' said the giant again.

'Yesterday master talked of this Mastermaid, and today it's the same story,' said the prince, who pretended to be silly and stupid. 'Bless you, master! Why don't you show me the thing at once? I should so like to see it only once in my life.'

'Oh, if that's all,' said the giant, 'you'll see her soon enough.'

The third day, at dawn, the giant went off to the wood again with his goats; but before he went he said to the prince: 'Today you must go to Hell and fetch my fire-tax. When you have done that you can rest yourself all day, for you must know it is an easy master you have come to.' And with that off he went.

'Easy master, indeed!' said the prince. 'You may be easy, but you set me hard tasks all the same. But I may as well see if I can find your Mastermaid, as you call her. I daresay she'll tell me what to do.' And so in he went to her again.

So when the Mastermaid asked what the giant had set him to do that day, he told her how he was to go to Hell and fetch the fire-tax.

'And how will you set about it?' asked the Mastermaid.

'Oh, that you must tell me,' said the prince. 'I have never been to Hell in my life; and even if I knew the way, I don't know how much I am to ask for.'

'Well, I'll soon tell you,' said the Mastermaid. 'You must go to the steep rock away yonder, under the hillside, and take the club that lies there, and knock on the face of the rock. Then there will come out one all glistening with fire; to him you must tell your errand, and when he asks you how much you will have, mind you say, "As much as I can carry."'

Yes, he would be sure to say that. So he sat in there with the Mastermaid all that day too; and though evening drew on, he would have sat there till now, had not the Mastermaid put him in mind that it was high time to be off to Hell to fetch the giant's fire-tax before he came home. So he went on his way, and did just as the Mastermaid had told him; and when he reached the rock, he took up the club and gave a great thump. Then the rock opened, and out came one whose face glistened, and out of whose eyes and nostrils flew sparks of fire.

'What is your will?' said he.

'Oh! I'm only come from the giant to fetch his fire-tax,' said the prince.

'How much will you have then?' asked the other.

'I never wish for more than I am able to carry,' said the prince.

'Lucky for you that you did not ask for a whole horse-load,' said he who came out of the rock, 'but come now into the rock with me, and you shall have it.'

So the prince went in with him, and you may fancy what heaps and heaps of gold and silver he saw lying in there, just like stones in a gravel pit; and he got a load just as big as he was able to carry, and set off home with it. Now, when the giant came home with his goats at even, the prince went into his room, and began to carol and sing as he had done the evenings before.

'Have you been to Hell after my fire-tax?' roared the giant.

'Oh yes, that I have, master,' answered the prince.

'Where have you put it?' asked the giant.

'There stands the sack on the bench yonder,' said the prince.

'I'll soon see to that,' said the giant, who strode off to the bench; and there he saw the sack so full that the gold and silver dropped out on the floor as soon as ever he untied the string.

'You've been talking to my Mastermaid, that I can see,' said the giant; 'but if you have, I'll wring your head off.'

'Mastermaid!' said the prince. 'Yesterday master talked of this Mastermaid, and today he talks of her again, and the day before yesterday it was the same story. I only wish I could see what sort of thing she is, that I do!'

'Well, well, wait till tomorrow,' said the giant, 'and then I'll take you in to her myself.'

'Thank you kindly, master,' said the prince, 'but it's only a joke of master's, I'll be bound.'

So next day the giant took him in to the Mastermaid, and said to her:

'Now, you must cut his throat, and boil him in the great big pot you wot of; and when the broth is ready, just give me a call.'

After that, he laid him down on the bench to sleep, and began to snore so that it sounded like thunder on the hills.

So the Mastermaid took a knife and cut the prince in his little finger, and let three drops of blood fall on a three-legged stool; and after that she took all the old rags, and soles of shoes, and all the rubbish she could lay hands on, and put them into the pot; and then she filled a chest full of ground gold, and took a lump of salt, and a flask of water that hung behind the door, and she took, besides, a golden apple, and two golden chickens, and off she set with the prince from the giant's house as fast as they could; and when they had gone a little way, they came to the sea, and after that they sailed over the sea; but where they got the ship from, I have never heard tell.

So when the giant had slumbered a good bit, he began to stretch himself as he lay on the bench and called out, 'Will it be soon done?'

'Only just begun,' answered the first drop of blood on the stool.

So the giant lay down to sleep again, and slumbered a long, long time. At last he began to toss about a little, and cried out, 'Do you hear what I say; will it be soon done?' but he did not look up this time, any more than the first, for he was still half asleep.

'Half done,' said the second drop of blood.

Then the giant thought again it was the Mastermaid, so he turned over on his other side, and fell asleep again. And when he had gone on sleeping for many hours, he began to stir and stretch his old bones, and to call out, 'Isn't it done yet?'

'Done to a turn,' said the third drop of blood.

Then the giant rose up and began to rub his eyes, but he couldn't see who it was that was talking to him, so he searched and called for the Mastermaid, but no one answered.

'Ah, well! I dare say she's just run out of doors for a bit,' he thought, and took up a spoon and went up to the pot to taste the broth; but he found nothing but shoe soles, and rags, and such stuff; and it was all boiled up together, so that he couldn't tell which was thick and which was thin. As soon as he saw this, he could tell how things had gone, and he got so angry he scarce knew which leg to stand upon. Away he went after the prince and the Mastermaid, till the wind whistled behind him; but before long, he came to the water and couldn't cross it.

'Never mind,' he said; 'I know a cure for this. I've only got to call on my stream-sucker.'

So he called on his stream-sucker, and he came and stooped down, and took one, two, three gulps; and then the water fell so much in the sea, that the giant could see the Mastermaid and the prince sailing in their ship.

'Now you must cast out the lump of salt,' said the Mastermaid.

So the prince threw it overboard, and it grew up into a mountain so high, right across the sea, that the giant couldn't pass it, and the stream-sucker couldn't help him by swilling any more water.

'Never mind!' cried the giant, 'there's a cure for this too.' So he called on his hill-borer to come and bore through the mountain, that the stream-sucker might creep through and take another swill; but just as they had made a hole through the hill, and the stream-sucker was about to drink, the Mastermaid told the prince to throw overboard a drop or two out of the flask, and then the sea was just as full as ever, and before the stream-sucker could take another gulp, they reached the land and were saved from the giant.

So they made up their minds to go home to the prince's father, but the prince would not hear of the Mastermaid's walking, for he thought it seemly neither for her nor for him.

'Just wait here ten minutes,' he said, 'while I go home after the seven horses which stand in my father's stall. It's no great way off, and I shan't be long about it; but I will not hear of my sweetheart walking to my father's palace.'

'Ah!' said the Mastermaid, 'pray don't leave me, for if you once get home to the palace, you'll forget me outright, I know you will.'

'Oh!' said he, 'how can I forget you; you with whom I have gone through so much, and whom I love so dearly?'

There was no help for it, he must and would go home to fetch the coach and seven horses, and she was to wait for him by the seaside. So at last the Mastermaid was forced to let him have his way. She only said, 'Now, when you get home, don't stop so much as to say good day to anyone, but go straight to the stable and put to the horses, and drive back as quick as you can; for they will all come about you, but do as though you did not see them. And above all things, mind you do not taste a morsel of food, for if you do, we shall both come to grief.'

All this the prince promised, but he thought all the time there was little fear of his forgetting her.

Now, just as he came home to the palace, one of his brothers was thinking of holding his bridal feast, and the bride, and all her kith and kin, were just come to the palace. So they all thronged round him, and asked about this thing and that, and wanted him to go in with them; but he made as though he did not see them, and went straight to the stall and got out the horses, and began to put them to. And when they saw they could not get him to go in, they came out to him with meat and drink, and the best of everything they had got ready for the feast; but the prince would not taste so much as a crumb, and put to as fast as he could. At last the bride's sister rolled an apple across the yard to him, saying, 'Well, if you won't eat anything else, you may as well take a bite of this, for you must be both hungry and thirsty after so long a journey.'

So he took up the apple and bit a piece out of it; but he had scarce done so, before he forgot the Mastermaid, and how he was to drive back for her.

'Well, I think I must be mad,' he said; 'what am I to do with this coach and horses?' So he put the horses up again, and went along with the others into the palace, and it was soon settled that he should have the bride's sister, who had rolled the apple over to him.

There sat the Mastermaid by the seashore, and waited and waited for the prince, but no prince came; so at last she went up from the shore, and after she had gone a bit she came to a little hut which lay by itself in a copse close by the king's palace. She went in and asked if she might lodge there. It was an old dame that owned the hut, and a cross-grained scolding hag she was as ever you saw. At first she would not hear of the Mastermaid's lodging in her house, but at last, for fair words and high rent, the Mastermaid got leave to be there. Now the hut was as dark and dirty as a pigsty, so the Mastermaid said she would smarten it up a little, that their house might look inside like other people's. The old hag did not like this either, and showed her teeth, and was cross, but the Mastermaid did not mind her. She took her chest of gold, and threw a handful or so into the fire, and lo, the gold melted, and bubbled and boiled over out of the grate, and spread itself over the whole hut, till it was gilded both outside and in. But as soon as the gold began to bubble and boil, the old hag got so afraid that she tried to run out as if the Evil One were at her heels; and as she ran out at the door, she forgot to stoop, and gave her head such a knock against the lintel that she broke her neck, and that was the end of her.

Next morning, the Constable passed that way, and you may fancy he could scarce believe his eyes when he saw the golden hut shining and glistening away in the copse; but he was still more astonished when he went in and saw the lovely maiden who sat there. To make a long story short, he fell over head and ears in love with her, and begged and prayed her to become his wife.

'Well, but have you much money?' asked the Mastermaid.

Yes, for that matter, he said, he was not so badly off, and off he went home to fetch the money, and when he came back at even he brought a half-bushel sack, and set it down on the bench. So the Mastermaid said she would have him, since he was so rich, but they were scarce in bed before she said she must get up again, 'For I have forgotten to make up the fire.'

'Pray, don't stir out of bed,' said the Constable; 'I'll see to it.'

So he jumped out of bed, and stood on the hearth in a trice.

'As soon as you have got hold of the shovel, just tell me,' said the Mastermaid.

'Well, I am holding it now,' said the Constable.

Then the Mastermaid said: 'God grant that you may hold the shovel, and the shovel you, and may you heap hot burning coals over yourself till morning breaks.'

So there stood the Constable all night long, shovelling hot burning coals over himself; and though he begged, and prayed, and wept, the coals were not a bit colder for that; but as soon as day broke, and he had power to cast away the shovel, he did not stay long, as you may fancy, but set off as if the Evil One or the bailiff were at his heels; and all who met him stared their eyes out at him, for he cut capers as though he were mad, and he could not have looked in worse plight if he had been flayed and tanned, and everyone wondered what had befallen him, but he told no one where he had been, for shame's sake.

Next day, the Attorney passed by the place where the Mastermaid lived, and he, too, saw how it shone and glistened in the copse. So he turned aside to find out who owned the hut, and when he came in and saw the lovely maiden, he fell more in love with her than the Constable, and began to woo her in hot haste.

Well, the Mastermaid asked him, as she had asked the Constable, if he had a good lot of money, and the Attorney said he wasn't so badly off; and as a proof he went home to fetch his money. So at even he came back with a great fat sack of money – I think it was a whole bushel sack – and set it down on the bench; and the long and the short of the matter was, that he was to have her, and they went to bed. But all at once the Mastermaid had forgotten to shut the door of the porch, and she must get up and make it fast for the night.

'What, you do that!' exclaimed the Attorney, 'while I lie here; that can never be; lie still, while I go and do it.'

So up he jumped, like a pea on a drum-head, and ran out into the porch.

'Tell me,' said the Mastermaid, 'when you have hold of the door latch.'

'I've got hold of it now,' said the Attorney.

'God grant, then,' said the Mastermaid, 'that you may hold the door, and the door you, and that you may go from wall to wall till day dawns.'

So you may fancy what a dance the Attorney had all night long; such a waltz he never had before, and I don't think he would much care if he never had such a waltz again. Now he pulled the door forward, and then the door pulled him back, and so he went on, now dashed into one corner of the porch, and now into the other, till he was almost battered to death. At first he began to curse and swear, and then to beg and pray, but the door cared for nothing but holding its own till break of day. As soon as it let go its hold, off set the Attorney, leaving behind him his money to pay for his night's lodging, and forgetting his courtship altogether, for to tell the truth, he was afraid lest the house door should come dancing after him. All who met him stared and gaped at him, for he, too, cut capers like a madman, and he could not have looked in worse plight if he had spent the whole night in butting against a flock of rams.

The third day, the Sheriff passed that way, and he, too, saw the golden hut, and turned aside to find out who lived there; and he had scarce set eyes on the Mastermaid, before he began to woo her. So she answered him as she had answered the other two. If he had lots of money she would have him, if not, he might go about his business. Well, the Sheriff said he wasn't so badly off, and he would go home and fetch the money, and when he came again at even, he had a bigger sack even than the Attorney – it must have been at least a bushel and a half – and put it down on the bench. So it was soon settled that he was to have the Mastermaid, but they had scarce gone to bed before the Mastermaid said she had forgotten to bring home the calf from the meadow, so she must get up and drive him into the stall. Then the Sheriff swore by all the powers that should never be, and, stout and fat as he was, up he jumped as nimbly as a kitten.

'Well, only tell me when you've got hold of the calf's tail,' said the Mastermaid.

'Now I have hold of it,' said the Sheriff.

'God grant,' said the Mastermaid, 'that you may hold the calf's tail, and the calf's tail you, and that you may make a tour of the world together till day dawns.'

Well you may just fancy how the Sheriff had to stretch his legs; away they went, the calf and he, over high and low, across hill and dale, and the more the Sheriff cursed and swore, the faster the calf ran and jumped. At dawn of day the poor Sheriff was well nigh broken-winded, and so glad was he to let go the calf's tail that he forgot his sack of money and everything else. As he was a great man, he went a little slower than the Attorney and the Constable, but the slower he went the more time people had to gape and stare at him; and I must say they made good use of their time, for he was terribly tattered and torn after his dance with the calf.

Next day was fixed for the wedding at the palace, and the eldest brother was to drive to church with his bride, and the younger, who had lived with the giant, with the bride's sister. But when they had got into the coach, and were just going to drive off, one of the trace pins snapped off; and though they made at least three in its place, they all broke, from whatever sort of wood they were made. So time went on and on, and they couldn't get to church, and everyone grew very downcast. But all at once the Constable said, for he, too, was bidden to the wedding, that yonder away in the copse lived a maiden. 'And if you can only get her to lend you the handle of her shovel with which she makes up her fire, I know very well it will hold.'

Well, they sent a messenger on the spot, with such a pretty message to the maiden, to know if they couldn't get the loan of her shovel which the Constable had spoken of. And the maiden said they might have it, so they got a trace pin which wasn't likely to snap.

But all at once, just as they were driving off, the bottom of the coach tumbled to bits. So they set to work to make a new bottom as they best might; but it mattered not how many nails they put into it, nor of what wood they made it, for as soon as ever they got the bottom well into the coach and were driving off, snap it went in two again, and they were even worse off than when they lost the trace pin. Just then the Attorney said – for if the Constable was there, you may fancy the Attorney was there too: 'Away yonder, in the copse, lives a maiden, and if you could only get her to lend you one-half of her porch door, I know it can hold together.'

Well, they sent another message to the copse, and asked so prettily if they couldn't have the loan of the gilded porch door which the Attorney had talked of, and they got it on the spot. So they were just setting out, but now the horses were not strong enough to draw the coach, though there were six of them; then they put on eight, and ten, and twelve, but the more they put on, and the more the coachman whipped, the more the coach wouldn't stir an inch. By this time, it was far on in the day, and everyone about the palace was in doleful dumps, for to church they must go, and yet it looked as if they should never get there. So at last the Sheriff said that yonder, in the gilded hut, in the copse, lived a maiden, and if they could only get the loan of her calf, 'I know it can drag the coach, though it were as heavy as a mountain.'

Well they all thought it would look silly to be drawn to church by a calf, but there was no help for it, so they had to send a third time, and ask so prettily in the king's name, if he couldn't get the loan of the calf the Sheriff had spoken of, and the Mastermaid let them have it on the spot, for she was not going to say 'no' this time either. So they put the calf on before the horses, and waited to see if it would do any good, and away went the coach over high and low, and stock and stone, so that they could scarce draw their breath; sometimes they were on the ground, and sometimes up in the air, and when they reached the church, the calf began to run round and round it like a spinning jenny, so that they had hard work to get out of the coach and into the church. When they went back, it was the same story, only they went faster, and they reached the palace almost before they knew they had set out.

Now when they sat down to dinner, the prince who had served with the giant said he thought they ought to ask the maiden who had lent them her shovel handle and porch door, and calf, to come up to the palace.

'For,' said he, 'if we hadn't got these three things, we should have been sticking here still.'

Yes, the king thought that only fair and right, so he sent five of his best men down to the gilded hut to greet the maiden from the king, and to ask her if she would be so good as to come up and dine at the palace.

'Greet the king from me,' said the Mastermaid, 'and tell him, if he's too good to come to me, so am I too good to go to him.'

So the king had to go himself, and then the Mastermaid went up with him without more ado. And as the king thought she was more than she seemed to be, he sat her down in the highest seat by the side of the youngest bridegroom.

Now, when they had sat a little while at table, the Mastermaid took out her golden apple, and the golden cock and hen, which she had carried off from the giant, and put them down on the table before her, and the cock and hen began at once to peck at one another, and to fight for the golden apple.

'Oh, only look,' said the prince; 'see how those two strive for the apple.'

'Yes!' said the Mastermaid; 'so we two strove to get away that time when we were together in the hillside.'

Then the spell was broken, and the prince knew her again, and you may fancy how glad he was. But as for the witch who had rolled the apple over to him, he had her torn to pieces between twenty-four horses, so that there was not a bit of her left, and after that they held on with the wedding in real earnest; and though they were still stiff and footsore, the Constable, the Attorney and the Sheriff kept it up with the best of them.

THE COCK AND THE HEN THAT WENT TO THE DOVREFELL

BY G. W. DASENT

Once on a time there was a hen that had flown up and perched on an oak tree for the night. When the night came, she dreamed that unless she got to the Dovrefell, the world would come to an end. So that very minute she jumped down and set out on her way. When she had walked a bit she met a cock.

'Good day, Cocky-Locky,' said the hen.

'Good day, Henny-Penny,' said the cock. 'Whither away so early?'

'Oh, I'm going to the Dovrefell, that the world mayn't come to an end,' said the hen.

'Who told you that, Henny-Penny?' asked the cock.

'I sat in the oak and dreamt it last night,' said the hen.

'I'll go with you,' said the cock.

Well, they walked on a good bit and then they met a duck.

'Good day, Ducky-Lucky,' said the cock.

'Good day, Cocky-Locky,' said the duck. 'Whither away so early?'

'Oh, I'm going to the Dovrefell, that the world mayn't come to an end,' said the cock.

'Who told you that, Cocky-Locky?'

'Henny-Penny,' said the cock.

'Who told you that, Henny-Penny?' asked the duck.

'I sat in the oak and dreamt it last night,' said the hen.

'I'll go with you,' said the duck.

So they went off together and after a bit they met a goose.

'Good day, Goosey-Poosey,' said the duck.

'Good day, Ducky-Lucky,' said the goose. 'Whither away so early?'

'I'm going to the Dovrefell, that the world mayn't come to an end,' said the duck.

'Who told you that, Ducky-Lucky?' asked the goose.

'Cocky-Locky.'

'Who told you that, Cocky-Locky?'

'Henny-Penny.'

'How you do know that, Henny-Penny?' asked the goose.

'I sat in the oak and dreamt it last night, Goosey-Poosey,' said the hen.

'I'll go with you,' said the goose.

Now when they had all walked along for a bit, a fox met them.

'Good day, Foxsy-Cocksy,' said the goose.

'Good day, Goosey-Poosey.'

'Whither away, Foxy-Cocksy?'

'Whither away yourself, Goosey-Poosey?'

'I'm going to the Dovrefell that the world mayn't come to an end,' said the goose.

'Who told you that, Goosey-Poosey?' asked the fox.

'Ducky-Lucky.'

'Who told you that, Ducky-Lucky?'

'Cocky-Locky.'

'Who told you that, Cocky-Locky?'

'Henny-Penny.'

'How do you know that, Henny-Penny?'

'I sat in the oak and dreamt last night, that if we don't get to the Dovrefell, the world will come to an end,' said the hen.

'Stuff and nonsense,' said the fox, 'the world won't come to an end if you don't get thither. No, come home with me to my earth. That's far better, for it's warm and jolly there.'

Well, they went home with the fox to his earth, and when they got in, the fox laid on lots of fuel, so that they all got very sleepy.

The duck and the goose, they settled themselves down in a corner, but the cock and hen flew up on a post. So when the goose and duck were well asleep, the fox took the goose and laid him on the embers and roasted him. The hen smelt the strong roast meat and sprang up to a higher peg, and said, half asleep, 'Faugh, what a nasty smell, what a nasty smell!'

'Oh, stuff,' said the fox. 'It's only the smoke driven down the chimney; go to sleep again, and hold your tongue.' So the hen went off to sleep again.

Now the fox had hardly got the goose well down his throat, before he did the very same with the duck. He took and laid him on the embers and roasted him for a dainty bit. Then the hen woke up again, and sprung up to a higher peg still. 'Faugh, what a nasty smell, what a nasty smell!' She said again, and then she got her eyes open and came to see how the fox had eaten both the twain, goose and duck; so she flew up to the highest peg of all, and perched there, and peeped up through the chimney.

'Nay, nay; just see what a lovely lot of geese flying yonder,' she said to the fox.

Out ran the fox to fetch a fat roast. But while he was gone, the hen woke up the cock and told him how it had gone with Goosey-Poosey and Ducky-Lucky. And so, Cocky-Locky and

Henny-Penny flew out through the chimney, and if they hadn't got to the Dovrefell, it surely would have been all over with the world.

THE PRINCESS ON THE GLASS HILL

BY G. W. DASENT

Once on a time, there was a man who had a meadow, that lay high up on the hillside, and in the meadow was a barn, which he had built to keep his hay in. Now, I must tell you, there hadn't been much in the barn for the last year or two, for every St John's Eve, when the grass stood greenest and deepest, the meadow was eaten down to the very ground by the next morning, just as if a whole drove of sheep had been there feeding on it overnight. This happened once, and it happened twice; so at last the man grew weary of losing his crop of hay, and said to his sons – for he had three of them, and the youngest was nicknamed Boots, of course – that now one of them must just go and sleep in the barn in the outlying field when St John's night came, for it was too good a joke that his grass should be eaten, root and blade, this year, as it had been the last two years. So whichever of them went must keep a sharp lookout; that was what their father said.

Well, the eldest son was ready to go and watch the meadow; trust him for looking after the grass! It shouldn't be his fault if man or beast, or the fiend himself, got a blade of grass. So, when evening came, he set off to the barn, and lay down to sleep; but a little on in the night came such a clatter, and such an earthquake, that walls and roof shook, and groaned, and creaked; then up jumped the lad, and took to his heels as fast as ever he could; nor dared he once look round till he reached home; and as for the hay, why it was eaten up this year just as it had been twice before.

The next St John's Eve, the man said again, it would never do to lose all the grass in the outlying field year after year in this way, so one of his sons must just trudge off to watch it, and watch it well, too. Well, the next oldest son was ready to try his luck, so he set off, and lay down to sleep in the barn as his brother had done before him; but as the night wore on, there came on a rumbling and quaking of the earth, worse even than on the last St John's Eve, and when the lad heard it, he got frightened, and took to his heels as though he were running a race.

Next year the turn came to Boots; but when he made ready to go, the other two began to laugh and to make game of him, saying, 'You're just the man to watch the hay, that you are – you, who have done nothing all your life but sit in the ashes and toast yourself by the fire.'

But Boots did not care a pin for their chattering, and stumped away as evening drew on, up the hillside to the outlying field. There he went inside the barn and lay down; but in about an hour's time the barn began to groan and creak, so that it was dreadful to hear. 'Well,' said Boots to himself, 'if it isn't worse than this, I can stand it well enough.'

A little while after came another creak and an earthquake, so that the litter in the barn flew about the lad's ears. 'Oh!' said Boots to himself, 'if it isn't worse than this, I daresay I can stand it out.'

But just then came a third rumbling, and a third earthquake, so that the lad thought walls and roof were coming down on his head; but it passed off, and all was still as death about him.

'It'll come again, I'll be bound,' thought Boots, but no, it didn't come again; still it was, and still it stayed. But after he had lain a little while, he heard a noise as if a horse were standing just outside the barn door, and cropping the grass. He stole to the door and peeped through a chink, and there stood a horse feeding away. So big, and fat, and grand a horse, Boots had never set eyes on; by his side on the grass lay a saddle and bridle, and a full set of armour for a knight, all of brass, so bright that the light gleamed from it.

'Ho, ho!' thought the lad, 'it's you, is it, that eats up our hay? I'll soon put a spoke in your wheel, just see if I don't.'

So he lost no time, but took the steel out of his tinder-box, and threw it over the horse; then it had no power to stir from the spot, and became so tame that the lad could do what he liked with it. So he got on its back, and rode off with it to a place which no one knew of, and there he put up the horse. When he got home, his brothers laughed and asked how he had fared?

'You didn't lie long in the barn, even if you had the heart to go so far as the field.'

'Well,' said Boots, 'all I can say is, I lay in the barn till the sun rose, and neither saw nor heard anything. I can't think what there was in the barn to make you both so afraid.'

'A pretty story,' said his brothers; 'but we'll soon see how you have watched the meadow.' So they set off, but when they reached it, there stood the grass as deep and thick as it had been over night.

Well, the next St John's Eve it was the same story over again; neither of the elder brothers dared to go out to the outlying field to watch the crop; but Boots, he had the heart to go, and everything happened just as it had happened the year before.

First a clatter and an earthquake, then a greater clatter and another earthquake, and so on a third time; only this year the earthquakes were far worse than the year before. Then all at once everything was as still as death, and the lad heard how something was cropping the grass outside the barn door, so he stole to the door and peeped through a chink; and what do you think he saw? Why, another horse standing right up against the wall, and chewing and champing with might and main. It was far finer and fatter than that which came the year before, and it had a saddle on its back, and a bridle on its neck, and a full suit of mail for a knight lay by its side, all of silver, and as grand as you would wish to see.

'Ho ho!' said Boots to himself, 'it's you that gobbles up our hay, is it? I'll soon put a spoke in your wheel.' And with that he took the steel out of his tinder-box, and threw it over the horse's crest, which stood as still as a lamb. Well, the lad rode this horse, too, to the hiding place where he kept the other one, and after that he went home.

'I suppose you'll tell us,' said one of his brothers, 'there's a fine crop this year too, up in the hayfield.'

'Well, so there is,' said Boots, and off ran the others to see. And there stood the grass thick and deep, as it was the year before, but they didn't give Boots softer words for all that.

Now, when the third St John's Eve came, the two elder still hadn't the heart to lie out in the barn and watch the grass, for they had got so scared at heart the night they lay there before, that they couldn't get over the fright; but Boots, he dared to go, and, to make a long story short, the very same thing happened this time as had happened twice before. Three earthquakes came, one after the other, each worse than the one which went before, and when the last came, the lad danced about with the shock from one barn wall to the other. And after that, all at once, it was still as death. Now when he had lain a little while, he heard something tugging away at the grass outside the barn, so he stole again to the door-chink and peeped out, and there stood a horse close outside – far, far bigger and fatter than the two he had taken before.

'Ho, ho!' said the lad to himself, 'it's you, is it, that comes here eating up our hay? I'll soon stop that – I'll soon put a spoke in your wheel.' So he caught up his steel and threw it over the horse's neck, and in a trice it stood as if it were nailed to the ground, and Boots could do as he pleased with it. Then he rode off with it to the hiding place where he kept the other two, and then went home. When he got home, his two brothers made a game of him as they had done before, saying, they could see he had watched the grass well, for he looked for all the world as if he were walking in his sleep, and many other spiteful things they said, but Boots gave no heed to them, only asking them to go and see for themselves; and when they went, there stood the grass as fine and deep this time as it had been twice before.

Now, you must know that the king of the country where Boots lived had a daughter, whom he would only give to the man who could ride up over the hill of glass, for there was a high, high hill, all of glass, as smooth and slippery as ice, close by the king's palace. Upon the tip top of the hill the king's daughter was to sit, with three golden apples in her lap, and the man who could ride up and carry off the three golden apples, was to have half the kingdom, and the princess to wife. This the king had stuck up on all the church doors in his realm, and had given it out in many other kingdoms besides. Now, this princess was so lovely, that all who set eyes on her fell over head and ears in love with her whether they would or no. So I needn't tell you how all the princes and knights who heard of her were eager to win her to wife, and half the kingdom beside; and how they came riding from all parts of the world on high prancing horses, and clad in the grandest clothes, for there wasn't one of them who hadn't made up his mind that he, and he alone, was to win the princess.

So when the day of trial came, which the king had fixed, there was such a crowd of princes and knights under the glass hill, that it made one's head whirl to look at them; and everyone in the country who could even crawl along was off to the hill, for they all were eager to see the man who was to win the princess. So the two elder brothers set off with the rest; but as for Boots, they said outright he shouldn't go with them, for if they were seen with such a dirty changeling, all begrimed with smut from cleaning their shoes and sifting cinders in the dusthole, they said folk would make game of them.

'Very well,' said Boots, 'it's all one to me. I can go alone, and stand or fall by myself.'

Now when the two brothers came to the hill of glass, the knights and princes were all hard at it, riding their horses till they were all in a foam; but it was no good, by my troth; for as soon as ever the horses set foot on the hill, down they slipped, and there wasn't one who could get a yard or two up; and no wonder, for the hill was as smooth as a sheet of glass, and as steep as a house wall. But all were eager to have the princess and half the kingdom. So they rode and slipped, and slipped and rode, and still it was the same story over again. At last all their horses were so weary that they could scarce lift a leg, and in such a sweat that the lather dripped from them, and so the knights had to give up trying anymore. So the king was just thinking that he would proclaim a new trial for the next day, to see if they would have better luck, when all at once a knight came riding up on so brave a steed, that no one had ever seen the like of it in his born days, and the knight had mail of brass, and the horse a brass bit in his mouth, so bright that the sunbeams shone from it. Then all the others called out to him he might just as well spare himself the trouble of riding at the hill, for it would lead to no good; but he gave no heed to them, and put his horse at the hill, and went up it like nothing for a good way, about a third of the height; and when he had got so far, he turned his horse round and rode down again. So lovely a knight the princess thought she had never yet seen, and while he was riding, she sat and thought to herself: 'Would to heaven he might only come up and down the other side.'

And when she saw him turning back, she threw down one of the golden apples after him, and it rolled down into his shoe. But when he got to the bottom of the hill he rode off so fast that no one could tell what had become of him. That evening all the knights and princes were to go before the king, that he who had ridden so far up the hill might show the apple which the princess had thrown, but there was no one who had anything to show. One after the other they all came, but not a man of them could show the apple.

At even, the brothers of Boots came home too, and had such a long story to tell about the riding up the hill.

'First of all,' they said, 'there was not one of the whole lot who could get so much as a stride up, but at last came one who had a suit of brass mail, and a brass bridle and saddle, all so bright that the sun shone from them a mile off. He was a chap to ride, just! He rode a third of the way up the hill of glass, and he could easily have ridden the whole way up, if he chose, but he turned round and rode down, thinking, maybe, that was enough for once.'

'Oh! I should so like to have seen him, that I should,' said Boots, who sat by the fireside, and stuck his feet into the cinders, as was his wont.

'Oh!' said his brothers, 'you would, would you? You don't look fit to keep company with such high lords, nasty beast that you are, sitting there amongst the ashes.'

Next day, the brothers were all for setting off again, and Boots begged them this time, too, to let him go with them and see the riding, but no, they wouldn't have him at any price, he was too ugly and nasty, they said.

'Well, well!' said Boots, 'if I go at all, I must go by myself. I'm not afraid.'

So when the brothers got to the hill of glass, all the princes and knights began to ride again, and you may fancy they had taken care to shoe their horses sharp; but it was no good – they rode and slipped, and slipped and rode, just as they had done the day before, and there was not one who could get so far as a yard up the hill. And when they had worn out their horses, so that they could not stir a leg, they were all forced to give it up as a bad job. So the king thought he might as well proclaim that the riding should take place the day after for the last time, just to give them one chance more; but all at once it came across his mind that he might as well wait a little longer, to see if the knight in brass mail would come this day too. Well, they saw nothing of him, but all at once came one riding on a steed, far, far, braver and finer than that on which the knight in brass had ridden, and he had silver mail, and a silver saddle and bridle, all so bright that the sunbeams gleamed and glanced from them far away. Then the others shouted out to him again, saying, he might as well hold hard, and not try to ride up the hill, for all his trouble would be thrown away, but the knight paid no heed to them, and rode straight at the hill, and right up it, till he had gone two-thirds of the way, and then he wheeled his horse round and rode down again. To tell the truth, the princess liked him still better than the knight in brass, and she sat and wished he might only be able to come right up to the top, and down the other side; but when she saw him turning back, she threw the second apple after him, and it rolled down and fell into his shoe. But, as soon as ever he had come down from the hill of glass, he rode off so fast that no one could see what became of him.

At even, when all were to go in before the king and the princess, that he who had the golden apple might show it, in they went, one after the other, but there was no one who had any apple to show, and the two brothers, as they had done on the former day, went home and told how things had gone, and how all had ridden at the hill, and none got up.

'But, last of all,' they said, 'came one in a silver suit, and his horse had a silver saddle and a silver bridle. He was just a chap to ride, and he got two-thirds up the hill and then turned back. He was a fine fellow, and no mistake, and the princess threw the second gold apple to him.'

'Oh!' said Boots, 'I should so like to have seen him too, that I should.'

'A pretty story,' they said. 'Perhaps you think his coat of mail was as bright as the ashes you are always poking about, and sifting, you nasty, dirty beast.'

The third day, everything happened as it had happened the two days before. Boots begged to go and see the sight, but the two wouldn't hear of his going with them. When they got to the hill, there was no one who could get so much as a yard up it; and now all waited for the knight in silver mail, but they neither saw nor heard of him. At last came one riding on a steed, so brave that no one had ever seen his match; and the knight had a suit of golden mail, and a golden saddle and bridle, so wondrous bright that the sunbeams gleamed from them a mile off. The other knights and princes could not find time to call out to him not to try his luck, for they were amazed to see how grand he was. So he rode right at the hill, and tore up it like nothing, so that the princess hadn't even time to wish that he might get up the whole way. As soon as ever he reached the top, he took the third golden apple from the princess' lap, and then turned his horse and rode down again. As soon as he got down, he rode off at full speed, and was out of sight in no time.

Now, when the brothers got home at even, you may fancy what long stories they told, how the riding had gone off that day, and amongst other things, they had a deal to say about the knight in golden mail.

'He was just a chap to ride!' they said. 'So grand a knight isn't to be found in the wide world.'

'Oh!' said Boots, 'I should so like to have seen him, that I should.'

'Ah!' said his brothers, 'his mail shone a deal brighter than the glowing coals which you are always poking and digging at, nasty, dirty beast that you are.'

Next day, all the knights and princes were to pass before the king and the princess – it was too late to do so the night before,

I suppose – that he who had the gold apple might bring it forth; but one came after another, first the princes, and then the knights, and still no one could show the gold apple.

'Well,' said the king, 'someone must have it, for it was something that we all saw with our own eyes, how a man came and rode up and bore it off.'

So he commanded that everyone who was in the kingdom should come up to the palace and see if they could show the apple. Well they all came, one after another, but no one had the golden apple, and after a long time the two brothers of Boots came. They were the last of all, so the king asked them if there was no one else in the kingdom who hadn't come.

'Oh, yes,' said they. 'We have a brother, but he never carried off the golden apple. He hasn't stirred out of the dusthole on any of the three days.'

'Never mind that,' said the king. 'He may as well come up to the palace like the rest.'

So Boots had to go up to the palace.

'How, now,' said the king. 'Have you got the golden apple? Speak out!'

'Yes, I have,' said Boots. 'Here is the first, and here is the second, and here is the third too.' And with that he pulled all three golden apples out of his pocket, and at the same time threw off his sooty rags, and stood before them in his gleaming golden mail.

'Yes!' exclaimed the king. 'You shall have my daughter, and half my kingdom, for you well deserve both her and it.'

So they got ready for the wedding, and Boots got the princess to wife, and there was great merry-making at the bridal feast, you may fancy, for they could all be merry though they couldn't ride up the hill of glass. And all I can say is, if they haven't left off their merry-making yet, why, they're still at it.

THE MASTER-SMITH

BY G. W. DASENT

Once on a time, in the days when our Lord and St Peter used to wander on earth, they came to a smith's house. He had made a bargain with the Devil, that the fiend should have him after seven years, but during that time he was to be the master of all masters in his trade, and to this bargain both he and the Devil had signed their names. So he had stuck up in great letters over the door of his forge: *'Here dwells the Master over all Masters.'*

Now when our Lord passed by and saw that, he went in.

'Who are you?' he said to the Smith.

'Read what's written over the door,' said the Smith. 'But maybe you can't read writing. If so, you must wait till someone comes to help you.'

Before our Lord had time to answer him, a man came with his horse, which he begged the Smith to shoe.

'Might I have leave to shoe it?' asked our Lord.

'You may try, if you like,' said the Smith, 'you can't do it so badly that I shall not be able to make it right again.'

So our Lord went out and took one leg off the horse, and laid it in the furnace, and made the shoe red-hot; after that, he turned up the ends of the shoe, and filed down the heads of the nails, and clenched the points; and then he put back the leg safe and sound on the horse again. And when he was done with that leg, he took the other foreleg and did the same with it; and when he was done with that, he took the hind legs – first, the off, and then the near leg – and laid them in the furnace, making the shoes red-hot, turning up the ends, filing the heads of the nails, and clenching the points; and after all was done, putting the legs on the horse again. All the while, the Smith stood by and looked on.

'You're not so bad a smith after all,' said he.

'Oh, you think so, do you?' said our Lord.

A little while after came the Smith's mother to the forge, and called him to come home and eat his dinner; she was an old, old woman with an ugly crook on her back and wrinkles in her face, and it was as much as she could do to crawl along.

'Mark now, what you see,' said our Lord.

Then he took the woman and laid her in the furnace, and smithied a lovely young maiden out of her.

'Well,' said the Smith, 'I say now, as I said before, you are not such a bad smith after all. There it stands over my door. *Here dwells the Master over all Masters*; but for all that, I say right out, one learns as long as one lives.' And with that he walked off to his house and ate his dinner.

So after dinner, just after he had got back to his forge, a man came riding up to have his horse shod.

'It shall be done in the twinkling of an eye,' said the Smith, 'for I have just learnt a new way to shoe, and a very good way it is when the days are short.'

So he began to cut and hack till he had got all the horse's legs off, for he said, I don't know why one should go pottering backwards and forwards – first, with one leg, and then with another.

Then he laid the legs in the furnace, just as he had seen our Lord lay them, and threw on a great heap of coal, and made his mates work the bellows bravely; but it went as one might suppose it would go. The legs were burnt to ashes, and the Smith had to pay for the horse.

Well, he didn't care much about that, but just then an old beggar-woman came along the road, and he thought to himself, 'better luck next time.' So he took the old dame and laid her in the furnace, and though she begged and prayed hard for her life, it was no good.

'You're so old, you don't know what is good for you,' said the Smith. 'Now you shall be a lovely young maiden in half no time, and for all that, I'll not charge you a penny for the job.'

But it went no better with the poor old woman than with the horse's legs.

'That was ill done, and I say it,' said our Lord.

'Oh! for that matter,' said the Smith, 'there's not many who'll ask after her, I'll be bound; but it's a shame of the Devil, if this is the way he holds to what is written up over the door.'

'If you might have three wishes from me,' said our Lord, 'what would you wish for?'

'Only try me,' said the Smith, 'and you'll soon know.'

So our Lord gave him three wishes.

'Well,' said the Smith, 'first and foremost, I wish that anyone whom I ask to climb up into the pear tree that stands outside by the wall of my forge, may stay sitting there till I ask him to come down again. The second wish I wish is that anyone whom I ask to sit down in my easy chair which stands inside the workshop yonder, may stay sitting there till I ask him to get up. Last of all, I wish that anyone whom I ask to creep into the steel purse which I have in my pocket, may stay in it till I give him leave to creep out again.'

'You have wished as a wicked man,' said St Peter. 'First and foremost, you should have wished for God's grace and goodwill.'

'I durstn't look so high as that,' said the Smith; and after that our Lord and St Peter bade him 'goodbye', and went on their way.

Well, the years went on and on, and when the time was up, the Devil came to fetch the Smith, as it was written in their bargain.

'Are you ready?' he asked, as he stuck his nose in at the door of the forge.

'Oh,' said the Smith, 'I must just hammer the head of this tenpenny nail first; meantime, you can just climb up into the pear tree, and pluck yourself a pear to gnaw at; you must be, both hungry and thirsty after your journey.'

So the Devil thanked him for his kind offer, and climbed up into the pear tree.

'Very good,' said the Smith; 'but now, on thinking the matter over, I find I shall never be able to have done hammering the head of this nail till four years are out at least – this iron is so plaguey hard. Down you can't come in all that time, but may sit up there and rest your bones.'

When the Devil heard this, he begged and prayed till his voice was as thin as a silver penny that he might have leave to come down, but there was no help for it. There he was, and there he must stay. At last he had to give his word of honour not to come again till the four years were out, which the Smith had spoken of, and then the Smith said, 'Very well, now you may come down.'

So when the time was up, the Devil came again to fetch the Smith. 'You're ready now, of course,' said he. 'You've had time enough to hammer the head of that nail, I should think.'

'Yes, the head is right enough now,' said the Smith. 'But still you have come a little tiny bit too soon, for I haven't quite done sharpening the point; such plaguey hard iron I never hammered in all my born days. So while I work at the point, you may just as well sit down in my easy chair and rest yourself; I'll be bound you're weary after coming so far.'

'Thank you kindly,' said the Devil, and down he plumped into the easy chair; but just as he had made himself comfortable, the Smith said, on second thoughts, he found he couldn't get the point sharp till four years were out. First of all, the Devil begged so prettily to be let out of the chair, and afterwards, waxing wroth, he began to threaten and scold, but the Smith kept on, all the while excusing himself, and saying it was all the iron's fault, it was so plaguy hard, and telling the Devil he was not so badly off to have to sit quietly in an easy chair, and that he would let him out to the minute when the four years were over. Well, at last there was no help for it, and the Devil had to give his word of honour not to fetch the Smith till the four years were out; and then the Smith said:

'Well now, you may get up and be off about your business,' and away went the Devil as fast as he could lay legs to the ground.

When the four years were over, the Devil came again to fetch the Smith, and he called out, as he stuck his nose in at the door of the forge: 'Now, I know you must be ready.'

'Ready, aye, ready,' answered the Smith; 'we can go now as soon as you please; but hark ye, there is one thing I have stood here and thought, and thought, I would ask you to tell me. Is it true what people say, that the Devil can make himself as small as he pleases?'

'God knows, it is the very truth,' said the Devil.

'Oh!' said the Smith; 'it *is* true, is it? Then I wish you would just be so good as to creep into this steel purse of mine, and see whether it is sound at the bottom, for to tell you the truth, I'm afraid my travelling money will drop out.'

'With all my heart,' said the Devil, who made himself small in a trice, and crept into the purse. But he was scarce in when the Smith snapped to the clasp.

'Yes,' called out the Devil inside the purse, 'it's right and tight everywhere.'

'Very good,' said the Smith. 'I'm glad to hear you say so, but "more haste the worse speed", says the old saw, and "forewarned is forearmed", says another; so I'll just weld these links a little together, just for safety's sake.' And with that he laid the purse in the furnace and made it red-hot.

'AU! AU!' screamed the Devil. 'Are you mad? Don't you know I'm inside the purse?'

'Yes, I do!' said the Smith, 'but I can't help you, for another old saw says, "one must strike while the iron is hot".' And as he said this, he took up his sledge-hammer, laid the purse on the anvil, and let fly at it as hard as he could.

'AU! AU! AU!' bellowed the Devil, inside the purse. 'Dear friend, do let me out, and I'll never come near you again.'

'Very well!' said the Smith, 'now, I think, the links are pretty well welded, and you may come out.' So he unclasped the purse, and away went the Devil in such a hurry that he didn't once look behind him.

Now, some time after, it came across the Smith's mind that he had done a silly thing in making the Devil his enemy, for, he said to himself, 'If, as is like enough, they won't have me in the Kingdom of Heaven, I shall be in danger of being houseless, since

I've fallen out with him who rules over Hell.'

So he made up his mind it would be best to try to get either into Hell or Heaven, and to try at once, rather than to put it off any longer, so that he might know how things really stood. Then he threw his sledge-hammer over his shoulder and set off; and when he had gone a good bit of the way, he came to a place where two roads met, and where the path to the Kingdom of Heaven parts from the path that leads to Hell, and here he overtook a tailor, who was pelting along with his goose in his hand.

'Good day,' said the Smith, 'whither are you off to?'

'To the Kingdom of Heaven,' said the Tailor, 'if I can only get into it – but whither are you going yourself?'

'Oh, our ways don't run together,' said the Smith, 'for I have made up my mind to try first in Hell, as the Devil and I know something of one another, from old times.'

So they bade one another 'Goodbye', and each went his way; but the Smith was a stout, strong man, and got over the ground far faster than the tailor, and so it wasn't long before he stood at the gates of Hell. Then he called the watch, and bade him go and tell the Devil there was someone outside who wished to speak a word with him.

'Go out,' said the Devil to the watch, 'and ask him who he is?' So when the watch came and told him that, the Smith answered:

'Go and greet the Devil in my name, and say it is the Smith who owns the purse he wots of and beg him prettily to let me in at once, for I worked at my forge till noon, and I have had a long walk since.'

But when the Devil heard who it was, he charged the watch to go back and lock up all the nine locks on the gates of Hell.

'And, besides,' he said, 'you may as well put on a padlock, for if he only once gets in, he'll turn Hell topsy-turvy!'

'Well!' said the Smith to himself, when he saw them busy bolting up the gates, 'there's no lodging to be got here, that's plain, so I may as well try my luck in the kingdom of Heaven.' And with that he turned round and went back till he reached the crossroads, and then he went along the path the tailor had taken. And now, as he was cross at having gone backwards and forwards so far for no good, he strode along with all his might, and reached the gate of Heaven just as St Peter was opening it a very little, just enough to let the half-starved tailor slip in. The Smith was still six or seven strides off the gate, so he thought to himself, 'Now there's no time to be lost!' And, grasping his sledge-hammer, he hurled it into the opening of the door just as the tailor slunk in, and if the Smith didn't get in then, when the door was ajar, why I don't know what has become of him.

THE TWO STEP-SISTERS

BY G. W. DASENT

Once on a time, there was a couple, and each of them had a daughter by a former marriage. The woman's daughter was dull and lazy, and could never turn her hand to anything, and the man's daughter was brisk and ready; but somehow or other she could never do anything to her stepmother's liking, and both the woman and her daughter would have been glad to be rid of her.

So it fell one day the two girls were to go out and spin by the side of the well, and the woman's daughter had flax to spin, but the man's daughter got nothing to spin but bristles.

'I don't know how it is,' said the woman's daughter, 'you're always so quick and sharp, but still I'm not afraid to have a spinning match with you.'

Well, they agreed that she whose thread first snapped, should go down the well. So they span away, but just as they were hard at it, the man's daughter's thread broke, and she had to go down the well. But when she got to the bottom she saw far and wide around her a fair green mead, and she hadn't hurt herself at all.

So she walked on a bit, till she came to a hedge which she had to cross.

'Ah! don't tread hard on me, pray don't, and I'll help you another time, that I will,' said the hedge.

Then the lassie made herself as light as she could, and trode so carefully she scarce touched a twig.

So she went on a bit further, till she came to a brindled cow, which walked there with a milking-pail on her horns. 'Twas a large pretty cow, and her udder was so full and round.

'Ah, be so good as to milk me, pray,' said the cow; 'I'm so full of milk. Drink as much as you please, and throw the rest over my hoofs, and see if I don't help you some day.'

So the man's daughter did as the cow begged. As soon as she touched the teats, the milk spouted out into the pail. Then she drank till her thirst was slaked, and the rest she threw over the cow's hoofs, and the milking-pail she hung on her horns again.

So when she had gone a bit further, a big wether met her, which had such thick long wool, it hung down and draggled after him on the ground, and on one of his horns hung a great pair of shears.

'Ah, please clip off my wool,' said the sheep, 'for here I go about with all this wool, and catch up everything I meet, and besides, it's so warm, I'm almost choked. Take as much of the fleece as you please, and twist the rest round my neck, and see if I don't help you some day.'

Yes, she was willing enough, and the sheep lay down of himself on her lap, and kept quite still, and she clipped him so neatly, there wasn't a scratch on his skin. Then she took as much of the wool as she chose, and the rest she twisted round the neck of the sheep.

A little further on, she came to an apple tree, which was loaded with apples; all its branches were bowed to the ground, and leaning against the stem was a slender pole.

'Ah, do be so good as to pluck my apples off me,' said the tree, 'so that my branches may straighten themselves again, for it's bad work to stand so crooked; but when you beat them down, don't strike me too hard. Then eat as many as you please, lay the rest round my root, and see if I don't help you some day or other.'

Yes, she plucked all she could reach with her hands, and then she took the pole and knocked down the rest, and afterwards she ate her fill, and the rest she laid neatly round the root.

So she walked on a long, long way, and then she came to a great farm-house, where an old hag of the trolls lived with her daughter. There she turned in to ask if she could get a place.

'Oh!' said the old hag, 'it's no use your trying. We've had ever so many maids, but none of them was worth her salt.'

But she begged so prettily that they would just take her on trial, that at last they let her stay. So the old hag gave her a sieve, and bade her go and fetch water in it. She thought it strange to fetch water in a sieve, but still she went, and when she came to the well, the little birds began to sing,

Daub in clay,
Stuff in straw!
Daub in clay,
Stuff in straw.

Yes, she did so, and found she could carry water in a sieve well enough; but when she got home with the water, and the old witch saw the sieve, she cried out:

'THIS YOU HAVEN'T SUCKED OUT OF YOUR OWN BREAST.'

So the old witch said that now she might go into the byre to pitch out dung and milk kine; but when she got there, she found a pitchfork so long and heavy that she couldn't stir it, much less work with it. She didn't know at all what to do, or what to make of it, but the little birds sang again that she should take the broomstick and toss out a little with that, and all the rest of the dung would fly after it. So she did that, and as soon as ever she began with the broomstick, the byre was as clean as if it had been swept and washed.

Now she had to milk the kine, but they were so restless that they kicked and frisked; there was no getting near them to milk them.

But the little birds sang outside:

A little drop, a tiny sup,
For the little birds to drink it up.

Yes, she did that; she just milked a tiny drop, 'twas as much as she could, for the little birds outside; and then all the cows stood still and let her milk them. They neither kicked nor frisked; they didn't even lift a leg.

So when the old witch saw her coming in with the milk, she cried out:

'THIS YOU HAVEN'T SUCKED OUT OF YOUR OWN BREAST. BUT NOW JUST TAKE THIS BLACK WOOL AND WASH IT WHITE.'

This the lassie was at her wits' end to know how to do, for she had never seen or heard of anyone who could wash black wool white. Still she said nothing, but took the wool and went down with it to the well. There the little birds sang again and told her to take the wool and dip it into the great butt that stood there; and she did so, and out it came as white as snow.

'Well, I never!' said the old witch, when she came in with the wool, 'it's no good keeping you. You can do everything, and at last you'll be the plague of my life. We'd best part, so take your wages and be off.'

Then the old hag drew out three caskets, one red, one green and one blue, and of these the lassie was to choose one as wages for her service. Now she didn't know at all which to choose, but the little birds sang:

Don't take the red, don't take the green,
But take the blue, where may be seen
Three little crosses all in a row;
We saw the marks, and so we know.

So she took the blue casket, as the birds sang.

'Bad luck to you, then,' said the old witch. 'See if I don't make you pay for this!'

So when the man's daughter was just setting off, the old witch shot a red-hot bar of iron after her, but she sprang behind the door and hid herself, so that it missed her, for her friends, the little birds, had told her beforehand how to behave. Then she walked on and on as fast as ever she could; but when she got to the apple tree, she heard an awful clatter behind her on the road, and that was the old witch and her daughter coming after her.

So the lassie was so frightened and scared, she didn't know what to do.

'Come hither to me, lassie, do you hear,' said the apple tree, 'I'll help you; get under my branches and hide, for if they catch you, they'll tear you to death, and take the casket from you.'

Yes, she did so, and she had hardly hidden herself before up came the old witch and her daughter.

'Have you seen any lassie pass this way, you apple tree?' asked the old hag.

'Yes, yes,' said the apple tree. 'One ran by here an hour ago, but now she's got so far ahead, you'll never catch her up.'

So the old witch turned back and went home again. Then the lassie walked on a bit, but when she came just about where the sheep was, she heard an awful clatter beginning on the road behind her, and she didn't know what to do, she was so scared and frightened, for she knew well enough it was the old witch, who had thought better of it.

'Come hither to me, lassie,' said the Wether, 'and I'll help you. Hide yourself under my fleece, and then they'll not see you; else they'll take away the casket, and tear you to death.'

Just then up came the old witch, tearing along.

'Have you seen any lassie pass here, you sheep?' she cried to the wether.

'Oh yes,' said the Wether, 'I saw one an hour ago, but she ran so fast, you'll never catch her.'

So the old witch turned round and went home.

But when the lassie had come to where she met the cow, she heard another awful clatter behind her.

'Come hither to me, lassie,' said the cow, 'and I'll help you to hide yourself under my udder, else the old hag will come and take away your casket, and tear you to death.'

True enough, it wasn't long before she came up.

'Have you seen any lassie pass here, you cow?' asked the old hag.

'Yes, I saw one an hour ago,' said the cow, 'but she's far away now, for she ran so fast I don't think you'll ever catch her up!'

So the old hag turned round, and went back home again.

When the lassie had walked a long, long way farther on, and was not far from the hedge, she heard again that awful clatter on the road behind her, and she got scared and frightened, for she knew well enough it was the old hag and her daughter, who had changed their minds.

'Come hither to me, lassie,' said the hedge, 'and I'll help you. Creep under my twigs, so that they can't see you; else they'll take the casket from you, and tear you to death.'

Yes, she made all the haste she could to get under the twigs of the hedge.

'Have you seen any lassie pass this way, you hedge?' asked the old hag to the hedge.

'No, I haven't seen any lassie,' answered the hedge, and was as smooth-tongued as if he had got melted butter in his mouth; but all the while he spread himself out, and made himself so big and tall, one had to think twice before crossing him. And so the old witch had no help for it but to turn round and go home again.

So when the man's daughter got home, her stepmother and her step-sister were more spiteful against her than ever; for now she was much neater, and so smart, it was a joy to look at her. Still she couldn't get leave to live with them, but they drove her out into a pigsty. That was to be her house. So she scrubbed it out so neat and clean, and then she opened her casket, just to see what she had got for her wages. But as soon as ever she unlocked it, she saw inside so much gold and silver, and lovely things, which came streaming out till all the walls were hung with them, and at last the pigsty was far grander than the grandest king's palace. And when the stepmother and her daughter came to see this, they almost jumped out of their skin, and began to ask what kind of a place she had down there?

'Oh,' said the lassie, 'can't you see, when I have got such good wages. 'Twas such a family, and such a mistress to serve, you couldn't find their like anywhere.'

Yes! The woman's daughter made up her mind to go out to serve too, that she might get just such another gold casket. So they sat down to spin again, and now the woman's daughter was to spin bristles, and the man's daughter flax, and she whose thread first snapped, was to go down the well. It wasn't long, as you may fancy, before the woman's daughter's thread snapped, and so they threw her down the well.

So the same thing happened. She fell to the bottom, but met with no harm, and found herself on a lovely green meadow. When she had walked a bit she came to the hedge. 'Don't tread hard on me, pray, lassie, and I'll help you again,' said the hedge.

'Oh!' said she, 'what should I care for a bundle of twigs?' and tramped and stamped over the hedge till it cracked and groaned again.

A little farther on she came to the cow, which walked about ready to burst for want of milking.

'Be so good as to milk me, lassie,' said the cow, 'and I'll help you again. Drink as much as you please, but throw the rest over my hoofs.'

Yes, she did that; she milked the cow, and drank till she could drink no more; but when she left off, there was none left to throw over the cow's hoofs, and as for the pail, she tossed it down the hill and walked on.

When she had gone a bit further, she came to the sheep which walked along with his wool dragging after him.

'Oh, be so good as to clip me, lassie,' said the sheep, 'and I'll serve you again. Take as much of the wool as you will, but twist the rest round my neck.'

Well! she did that; but she went so carelessly to work, that she cut great pieces out of the poor sheep, and as for the wool, she carried it all away with her.

A little while after she came to the apple tree, which stood there quite crooked with fruit again.

'Be so good as to pluck the apples off me, that my limbs may grow straight, for it's weary work to stand all awry,' said the apple tree. 'But please take care not to beat me too hard. Eat as many as you will, but lay the rest neatly round my root, and I'll help you again.'

Well, she plucked those nearest to her, and thrashed down those she couldn't reach with the pole, but she didn't care how she did it, and broke off and tore down great boughs, and ate till she was as full as full could be, and then she threw down the rest under the tree.

So when she had gone a good bit further, she came to the farm where the old witch lived. There she asked for a place, but the old hag said she wouldn't have any more maids, for they were either worth nothing, or were too clever, and cheated her out of her goods. But the woman's daughter was not to be put off, she *would* have a place, so the old witch said she'd give her a trial, if she was fit for anything.

The first thing she had to do was to fetch water in a sieve. Well, off she went to the well, and drew water in a sieve, but as fast as she got it in it ran out again. So the little birds sung:

Daub in clay,
Put in straw!
Daub in clay,
Put in straw!

But she didn't care to listen to the birds' song, and pelted them with clay, till they flew off far away. And so she had to go home with the empty sieve, and got well scolded by the old witch.

Then she was to go into the byre to clean it, and milk the kine. But she was too good for such dirty work, she thought. Still, she went out into the byre, but when she got there, she couldn't get on at all with the pitchfork, it was so big. The birds said the same to her as they had said to her step-sister, and told her to take the broomstick, and toss out a little dung, and then all the rest would fly after it; but all she did with the broomstick was to throw it at the birds. When she came to milk, the kine were so unruly, they kicked and pushed, and every time she got a little milk in the pail, over they kicked it. Then the birds sang again:

A little drop and a tiny sup
For the little birds to drink it up.

But she beat and banged the cows about, and threw and pelted at the birds everything she could lay hold of, and made such a to do, 'twas awful to see. So she didn't make much either of her pitching or milking, and when she came indoors she got blows as well as hard words from the old witch, who sent her off to wash the black wool white; but that, too, she did no better.

Then the old witch thought this really too bad, so she set out the three caskets, one red, one green and one blue, and said she'd no longer any need of her services, for she wasn't worth keeping, but for wages she should have leave to choose whichever casket she pleased.

Then sung the little birds:

Don't take the red, don't take the green,
But choose the blue, where may be seen
Three little crosses all in a row;
We saw the marks, and so we know.

She didn't care a pin for what the birds sang, but took the red, which caught her eye most. And so she set out on her road home, and she went along quietly and easily enough; there was no one who came after *her*.

So when she got home, her mother was ready to jump with joy, and the two went at once into the ingle, and put the casket up there, for they made up their minds there could be nothing in it but pure silver and gold, and they thought to have all the walls and roof gilded like the pigsty. But lo, when they opened the casket there came tumbling out nothing but toads, and frogs, and snakes; and worse than that, whenever the woman's daughter opened her mouth, out popped a toad or a snake, and all the vermin one ever thought of, so that at last there was no living in the house with her.

That was all the wages *she* got for going out to service with the old witch.

TAMING THE SHREW

BY G. W. DASENT

Once on a time, there was a king, and he had a daughter who was such a scold, and whose tongue went so fast, there was no stopping it. So he gave out that the man who could stop her tongue should have the princess to wife, and half his kingdom into the bargain. Now, three brothers, who heard this, made up their minds to go and try their luck; and first of all the two elder went, for they thought they were the cleverest; but they couldn't cope with her at all, and got well thrashed besides.

Then Boots, the youngest, set off, and when he had gone a little way he found an ozier band lying on the road, and he picked it up. When he had gone a little farther he found a piece of a broken plate, and he picked that up too. A little farther on he found a dead magpie, and a little farther on still, a crooked ram's horn; so he went on a bit and found the fellow to the horn; and at last, just as he was crossing the fields by the king's palace, where they were pitching out dung, he found a worn-out shoe-sole. All these things he took with him into the palace, and went before the princess.

'Good day,' said he.

'Good day,' said she, and made a wry face.

'Can I get my magpie cooked here?' he asked.

'I'm afraid it will burst,' answered the princess.

'Oh, never fear! For I'll just tie this ozier band round it,' said the lad, as he pulled it out.

'The fat will run out of it,' said the princess.

'Then I'll hold this under it,' said the lad, and showed her the piece of broken plate.

'You are so crooked in your words,' said the princess, 'there's no knowing where to have you.'

'No, I'm not crooked,' said the lad; 'but this is,' as he held up one of the horns.

'Well!' said the princess, 'I never saw the match of this in all my days.'

'Why, here you see the match to it,' said the lad, as he pulled out the other ram's horn.

'I think,' said the princess, 'you must have come here to wear out my tongue with your nonsense.'

'No, I have not,' said the lad; 'but this is worn out,' as he pulled out the shoe sole.

To this the princess hadn't a word to say, for she had fairly lost her voice with rage.

'Now you are mine,' said the lad; and so he got the princess to wife, and half the kingdom.

SHORTSHANKS

BY G. W. DASENT

Once on a time, there was a poor couple who lived in a tumble down hut, in which there was nothing but black want, so that they hadn't a morsel to eat, nor a stick to burn. But though they had next to nothing of other things, they had God's blessing in the way of children, and every year they had another babe. Now, when this story begins, they were just looking out for a new child; and, to tell the truth, the husband was rather cross, and he was always going about grumbling and growling, and saying, that for his part, he thought one might have too many of these God's gifts. So when the time came that the babe was to be born, he went off into the wood to fetch fuel, saying that he didn't care to stop and see the young squaller; he'd be sure to hear him soon enough, screaming for food.

Now, when her husband was well out of the house, his wife gave birth to a beautiful boy, who began to look about the room as soon as ever he came into the world.

'Oh, dear mother,' he said, 'give me some of my brother's cast-off clothes, and a few days' food, and I'll go out into the world and try my luck; you have children enough as it is, that I can see.'

'God help you, my son!' answered his mother, 'that can never be. You are far too young yet.'

But the tiny one stuck to what he said, and begged and prayed till his mother was forced to let him have a few old rags, and a little food tied up in a bundle, and off he went right merrily and manfully into the wide world. But he was scarce out of the house before his mother had another boy, and he too looked about him, and said: ‘Oh, dear mother, give me some of my brother’s old clothes and a few days’ food, and I’ll go out into the world to find my twin-brother; you have children enough already on your hands, that I can see.’

‘God help you, my poor little fellow!’ said his mother, ‘you are far too little. This will never do.’

But it was no good; the tiny one begged and prayed so hard, till he got some old tattered rags and a bundle of food; and so he wandered out into the world like a man, to find his twin brother. Now, when the younger had walked a while, he saw his brother a good bit on before him, so he called out to him to stop.

‘Holloa! Can’t you stop? Why, you lay legs to the ground as if you were running a race. But you might just as well have stayed to see your youngest brother before you set off into the world in such a hurry.’

So the elder stopped and looked round; and when the younger had come up to him and told him the whole story, and how he was his brother, he went on to say: ‘But let’s sit down here and see what our mother has given us for food.’ So they sat down together, and were soon great friends.

Now when they had gone a bit farther on their way, they came to a brook which ran through a green meadow, and the youngest said now the time was come to give one another names: ‘Since we set off in such a hurry that we hadn’t time to do it at home, we may as well do it here.’

‘Well!’ said the elder, ‘and what shall your name be?’

‘Oh!’ said the younger, ‘my name shall be Shortshanks; and yours, what shall it be?’

'I will be called King Sturdy,' answered the eldest.

So they christened each other in the brook, and went on. But when they had walked a while they came to a crossroad, and agreed they should part there, and each take his own road. So they parted, but they hadn't gone half a mile before their roads met again. So they parted the second time, and took each a road; but in a little while the same thing happened, and they met again, they scarce knew how; and the same thing happened a third time also. Then they agreed that they should each choose a quarter of the heavens, and one was to go east and the other west. But before they parted, the elder said: 'If you ever fall into misfortune or need, call three times on me, and I will come and help you; but mind you don't call on me till you are at the last pinch.'

'Well!' said Shortshanks, 'if that's to be the rule, I don't think we shall meet again very soon.'

After that they bade each other goodbye, and Shortshanks went east and King Sturdy west.

Now, you must know, when Shortshanks had gone a good bit alone, he met an old, old crook-backed hag, who had only one eye, and Shortshanks snapped it up.

'Oh! oh!' screamed the hag, 'what has become of my eye?'

'What will you give me,' asked Shortshanks, 'if you get your eye back?'

'I'll give you a sword, and such a sword! It will put a whole army to flight, be it ever so great,' answered the old woman.

'Out with it, then!' said Shortshanks.

So the old hag gave him the sword, and got her eye back again. After that, Shortshanks wandered on a while, and another old, old crook-backed hag met him who had only one eye, which Shortshanks stole before she was aware of him.

'Oh, oh! whatever has become of my eye,' screamed the hag.

'What will you give me to get your eye back?' asked Shortshanks.

'I'll give you a ship,' said the woman, 'which can sail over fresh water and salt water, and over high hills and deep dales.'

'Well! out with it,' said Shortshanks.

So the old woman gave him a little tiny ship, no bigger than he could put in his pocket, and she got her eye back again, and they each went their way. But when he had wandered on a long, long way, he met a third time an old, old crook-backed hag, with only one eye. This eye, too, Shortshanks stole; and when the hag screamed and made a great to-do, bawling out what had become of her eye, Shortshanks said, 'What will you give me to get back your eye?'

Then she answered: 'I'll give you the art how to brew a hundred lasts of malt at one strike.'

Well, for teaching that art the old hag got back her eye, and they each went their way.

But when Shortshanks had walked a little way, he thought it might be worthwhile to try his ship; so he took it out of his pocket, and put first one foot into it, and then the other; and as soon as ever he set one foot into it, it began to grow bigger and bigger, and by the time he set the other foot into it, it was as big as other ships that sail on the sea. Then Shortshanks said: 'Off and away, over fresh water and salt water, over high hills and deep dales, and don't stop till you come to the king's palace.'

And lo, away went the ship as swiftly as a bird through the air, till it came down a little below the king's palace, and there it stopped. From the palace windows people had stood and seen Shortshanks come sailing along, and they were all so amazed that they ran down to see who it could be that came sailing in a ship through the air. But while they were running down, Shortshanks had stepped out of his ship and put it into his pocket again; for as soon as he stepped out of it, it became as small as it was when he got it from the old woman. So those who had run down from the palace saw no one but a ragged little boy standing down there by the strand. Then the king asked whence he came, but the boy said he didn't know, nor could he tell them how he had got there. There he was, and that was all they could get out of him. But he begged and prayed so prettily to get a place in the king's palace, saying, if there was nothing else for him to do, he could carry in wood and water for the kitchen maid, that their hearts were touched, and he got leave to stay there.

Now when Shortshanks came up to the palace, he saw how it was all hung with black, both outside and in, wall and roof, so he asked the kitchen maid what all that mourning meant?

'Don't you know?' said the kitchen maid, 'I'll soon tell you. The king's daughter was promised away a long time ago to three ogres, and next Thursday evening one of them is coming to fetch her. Ritter Red, it is true, has given out that he is man enough to set her free, but God knows if he can do it. And now you know why we are all in grief and sorrow.'

So when Thursday evening came, Ritter Red led the princess down to the strand, for there it was she was to meet the ogre, and he was to stay by her there and watch; but he wasn't likely to do the ogre much harm, I reckon, for as soon as ever the princess had sat down on the strand, Ritter Red climbed up into a great tree that stood there, and hid himself as well as he could among the boughs. The princess begged and prayed him not to leave her, but Ritter Red turned a deaf ear to her, and all he said was, 'Tis better for one to lose life than for two.' That was what Ritter Red said.

Meantime, Shortshanks went to the kitchen maid, and asked her so prettily if he mightn't go down to the strand for a bit?

'And what should take you down to the strand?' asked the kitchen maid. 'You know you've no business there.'

'Oh, dear friend,' said Shortshanks. 'Do let me go, I should so like to run down there and play a while with the other children; that I should.'

'Well, well!' said the kitchen maid, 'off with you, but don't let me catch you staying there a bit over the time when the brose for supper must be set on the fire, and the roast put on the spit; and let me see, when you come back, mind you bring a good armful of wood with you.'

Yes, Shortshanks would mind all that. So off he ran down to the strand.

But just as he reached the spot where the princess sat, what should come but the ogre tearing along in his ship, so that the wind roared and howled after him. He was so tall and stout it was awful to look on him, and he had five heads of his own.

'Fire and flame!' screamed the ogre.

'Fire and flame yourself!' said Shortshanks.

'Can you fight?' roared the ogre.

'If I can't, I can learn,' said Shortshanks.

So the ogre struck at him with a great thick iron club which he had in his fist, and the earth and stones flew up five yards into the air after the stroke.

'My!' said Shortshanks, 'that was something like a blow, but now you shall see a stroke of mine.'

Then he grasped the sword he had got from the old crook-backed hag, and cut at the ogre; and away went all his five heads flying over the sand. So when the princess saw she was saved, she was so glad that she scarce knew what to do, and she jumped and danced for joy. 'Come, lie down, and sleep a little in my lap,' she said to Shortshanks, and as he slept she threw over him a tinsel robe.

Now you must know, it wasn't long before Ritter Red crept down from the tree, as soon as he saw there was nothing to fear in the way, and he went up to the princess and threatened her until she promised to say it was he who had saved her life; for if she wouldn't say so, he said he would kill her on the spot. After that he cut out the ogre's lungs and tongue, and wrapped them up in his handkerchief, and so led the princess back to the palace, and whatever honours he had not before, he got then, for the king did not know how to find honour enough for him, and made him sit every day on his right hand at dinner.

As for Shortshanks, he went first of all on board the ogre's ship, and took a whole heap of gold and silver rings, as large as hoops, and trotted off with them as hard as he could to the palace. When the kitchen maid set her eyes on all that gold and silver, she was quite scared, and asked him, 'But dear, good, Shortshanks, wherever did you get all this from?' For she was rather afraid he hadn't come rightly by it.

'Oh!' answered Shortshanks, 'I went home for a bit, and there I found these hoops, which had fallen off some old pails of ours, so I laid hands on them for you, if you must know.'

Well, when the kitchen maid heard they were for her, she said nothing more about the matter, but thanked Shortshanks, and they were good friends again.

The next Thursday evening it was the same story over again; all were in grief and trouble, but Ritter Red said, as he had saved the princess from one ogre, it was hard if he couldn't save her from another; and down he led her to the strand as brave as a lion. But he didn't do this ogre much harm either, for when the time came that they looked for the ogre, he said, as he had said before, ''Tis better one should lose life than two,' and crept up into his tree again. But Shortshanks begged the kitchen maid to let him go down to the strand for a little.

'Oh!' said the kitchen maid, 'and what business have you down there?'

'Dear friend,' said Shortshanks, 'do pray let me go. I long so to run down and play a while with the other children.'

Well, the kitchen maid gave him leave to go, but he must promise to be back by the time the roast was turned, and he was to mind and bring a big bundle of wood with him. So Shortshanks had scarce got down to the strand, when the ogre came tearing along in his ship, so that the wind howled and roared around him; he was twice as big as the other ogre, and he had ten heads on his shoulders.

'Fire and flame!' screamed the ogre.

Fire and flame yourself!' answered Shortshanks.

'Can you fight?' roared the ogre.

'If I can't, I can learn,' said Shortshanks.

Then the ogre struck at him with his iron club; it was even bigger than that which the first ogre had, and the earth and stones flew up ten yards into the air.

My!' said Shortshanks, 'that was something like a blow, but now you shall see a stroke of mine.' Then he grasped his sword, and cut off all the ogre's ten heads at one blow, and sent them dancing away over the sand.

Then the princess said again to him, 'Lie down and sleep a little while on my lap.' And while Shortshanks lay there, she threw over him a silver robe. But as soon as Ritter Red marked that there was no more danger in the way, he crept down from the tree, and threatened the princess, till she was forced to give her word, to say it was he who had set her free. After that, he cut the lungs and tongue out of the ogre, and wrapped them in his handkerchief, and led the princess back to the palace. Then you may fancy what mirth and joy there was, and the king was at his wits' end to know how to show Ritter Red honour and favour enough.

This time, too, Shortshanks took a whole armful of gold and silver rings from the ogre's ship, and when he came back to the palace the kitchen maid clapped her hands in wonder, asking wherever he got all that gold and silver from. But Shortshanks answered that he had been home a while, and that the hoops had fallen off some old pails, so he had laid his hands on them for his friend the kitchen maid. So when the third Thursday evening came, everything happened as it had happened twice before; the whole palace was hung with black, and all went about mourning and weeping. But Ritter Red said he couldn't see what need they had to be so afraid; he had freed the princess from two ogres, and he could very well free her from a third. So he led her down to the strand, but when the time drew near for the ogre to come up, he crept into his tree again, and hid himself. The princess begged and prayed, but it was no good, for Ritter Red said again, ''Tis better that one should lose life than two.'

That evening, too, Shortshanks begged for leave to go down to the strand.

'Oh!' said the kitchen maid, 'what should take you down there?'

But he begged and prayed so, that at last he got leave to go, only he had to promise to be back in the kitchen again when the roast was to be turned. So off he went, but he had scarce reached the strand when the ogre came with the wind howling and roaring after him. He was much, much bigger than either of the other two, and he had fifteen heads on his shoulders.

'Fire and flame!' roared out the ogre.

'Fire and flame yourself!' said Shortshanks.

'Can you fight?' screamed the ogre.

'If I can't, I can learn,' said Shortshanks.

'I'll soon teach you,' screamed the ogre, and struck at him with his iron club, so that the earth and stones flew up fifteen yards into the air.

'My!' said Shortshanks, 'that was something like a blow, but now you shall see a stroke of mine.'

As he said that, he grasped his sword, and cut off all the ogre's fifteen heads at one blow, and sent them all dancing over the sand.

So the princess was freed from all the ogres, and she both blessed and thanked Shortshanks for saving her life.

'Sleep now a while on my lap,' she said; and he laid his head on her lap, and while he slept, she threw over him a golden robe.

'But how shall we let it be known that it is you that have saved me?' she asked, when he awoke.

'Oh, I'll soon tell you,' answered Shortshanks. 'When Ritter Red has led you home again, and given himself out as the man who has saved you, you know he is to have you to wife, and half the kingdom. Now, when they ask you, on your wedding day, whom you will have to be your cup-bearer, you must say, "I will have the ragged boy who does odd jobs in the kitchen, and carries in wood and water for the kitchen maid." So when I am filling your cups, I will spill a drop on his plate, but none on yours; then he will be wroth, and give me a blow, and the same thing will happen three times. But the third time you must mind and say, "Shame on you to strike my heart's darling! He it is who set me free, and him will I have!"'

After that, Shortshanks ran back to the palace as he had done before; but he went first on board the ogre's ship, and took a whole heap of gold, silver and precious stones, and out of them he gave the kitchen maid another great armful of gold and silver rings.

Well, as for Ritter Red, as soon as ever he saw that all risk was over, he crept down from his tree, and threatened the princess till she was forced to promise she would say it was he who had saved her. After that, he led her back to the palace, and all the honour shown him before was nothing to what he got now, for the king thought of nothing else than how he might best honour the man who had saved his daughter from the three ogres. As for his marrying her, and having half the kingdom, that was a settled thing, the king said. But when the wedding day came, the princess begged she might have the ragged boy who carried in wood and water for the cook to be her cup-bearer at the bridal feast.

'I can't think why you should want to bring that filthy beggar boy in here,' said Ritter Red. But the princess had a will of her own, and said she would have him, and no one else, to pour out her wine; so she had her way at last. Now everything went as it had been agreed between Shortshanks and the princess; he spilled a drop on Ritter Red's plate, but none on hers, and each time Ritter Red got wroth and struck him. At the first blow Shortshank's rags fell off which he had worn in the kitchen; at the second the tinsel robe fell off; and at the third the silver robe; and then he stood in his golden robe, all gleaming and glittering in the light. Then the princess said, 'Shame on you to strike my heart's darling! He has saved me, and him will I have!'

Ritter Red cursed and swore it was he who had set her free, but the king put in his word, and said: 'The man who saved my daughter must have some token to show for it.'

Yes, Ritter Red had something to show! And he ran off at once after his handkerchief with the lungs and tongues in it, and Shortshanks fetched all the gold and silver, and precious things, he had taken out of the ogres' ships. So each laid his tokens before the king, and the king said, 'The man who has such precious stores of gold, and silver, and diamonds, must have slain the ogre and spoiled his goods, for such things are not to be had elsewhere.'

So Ritter Red was thrown into a pit full of snakes, and Shortshanks was to have the princess and half the kingdom.

One day Shortshanks and the king were out walking, and Shortshanks asked the king if he hadn't any more children?

'Yes,' said the king, 'I had another daughter but the ogre has taken her away because there was no one who could save her. Now you are going to have one daughter, but if you can set the other free whom the ogre has carried off, you shall have her too with all my heart, and the other half of my kingdom.'

'Well,' said Shortshanks, 'I may as well try, but I must have an iron cable, five hundred fathoms long, and five hundred men, and food for them to last fifteen weeks, for I have a long voyage before me.'

Yes, the king said he should have them, but he was afraid there wasn't a ship in his kingdom big enough to carry such a freight.

'Oh! if that's all,' said Shortshanks, 'I have a ship of my own.'

With that he whipped out of his pocket the ship he had got from the old hag.

The king laughed, and thought it was all a joke, but Shortshanks begged him only to give him what he asked, and he should soon see if it was a joke. So they got together what he wanted, and Shortshanks bade him put the cable on board the ship first of all; but there was no one man who could lift it, and there wasn't room for more than one at a time round the tiny ship. Then Shortshanks took hold of the cable by one end, and laid a link or two into the ship; and as he threw in the links, the ship grew bigger and bigger, till at last it got so big, that there was room enough and to spare in it for the cable, and the five hundred men, and their food, and Shortshanks, and all. Then he said to the ship: 'Off and away, over fresh water and salt water, over high hill and deep dale, and don't stop till you come to where the king's daughter is.' And away went the ship over land and sea, till the wind whistled after it.

So when they had sailed far, far away, the ship stood stock still in the middle of the sea.

'Ah!' said Shortshanks, 'now we have got so far, but how we are to get back is another story.'

Then he took the cable and tied one end of it round his waist, and said: 'Now, I must go to the bottom, but when I give the cable a good tug, and want to come up again, mind you all hoist away with a will, or your lives will be lost as well as mine.' And with these words, overboard he leapt, and dived down, so that the yellow waves rose round him in an eddy.

Well, he sank and sank, and at last he came to the bottom, and there he saw a great rock rising up with a door in it, so he opened the door and went in. When he got inside, he saw another princess, who sat and sewed, but when she saw Shortshanks, she clasped her hands together and cried out: 'Now, God be thanked! you are the first Christian man I've set eyes on since I came here.'

'Very good,' said Shortshanks, 'but do you know I've come to fetch you?'

'Oh!' she cried, 'you'll never fetch me; you'll never have that luck, for if the ogre sees you, he'll kill you on the spot.'

'I'm glad you spoke of the ogre,' said Shortshanks ''twould be fine fun to see him. Whereabouts is he?'

Then the princess told him the ogre was out looking for someone who could brew a hundred lasts of malt at one strike, for he was going to give a great feast, and less drink wouldn't do.

'Well! I can do that,' said Shortshanks.

'Ah!' said the princess, 'if only the ogre wasn't so hasty, I might tell him about you. But he's so cross; I'm afraid he'll tear you to pieces as soon as he comes in, without waiting to hear my story. Let me see what is to be done. Oh! I have it; just hide yourself in the sideroom yonder, and let us take our chance.'

Well, Shortshanks did as she told him, and he had scarce crept into the sideroom before the ogre came in.

'HUF!' said the ogre, 'what a horrid smell of Christian man's blood!'

'Yes!' said the princess, 'I know there is, for a bird flew over the house with a Christian man's bone in his bill, and let it fall down the chimney. I made all the haste I could to get it out again, but I dare say it's that you smell.'

'Ah!' said the ogre, 'like enough.'

Then the princess asked the ogre if he had laid hold of anyone who could brew a hundred lasts of malt at one strike?

'No,' said the ogre, 'I can't hear of anyone who can do it.'

'Well,' she said, 'a while ago, there was a chap in here who said he could do it.'

'Just like you, with your wisdom!' said the ogre. 'Why did you let him go away then, when you knew he was the very man I wanted?'

'Well then, I didn't let him go,' said the princess. 'But father's temper is a little hot, so I hid him away in the sideroom yonder; but if father hasn't hit upon anyone, here he is.'

'Well,' said the ogre, 'let him come in then.'

So Shortshanks came in, and the ogre asked him if it were true that he could brew a hundred lasts of malt at a strike?

'Yes it is,' said Shortshanks.

'Twas good luck then to lay hands on you,' said the ogre, 'and now fall to work this minute; but heaven help you if you don't brew the ale strong enough.'

'Oh,' said Shortshanks, 'never fear, it shall be stinging stuff'; and with that he began to brew without more fuss, but all at once he cried out: 'I must have more of you ogres to help in the brewing, for these I have got a'nt half strong enough.'

Well, he got more – so many, that there was a whole swarm of them, and then the brewing went on bravely. Now when the sweetwort was ready, they were all eager to taste it, you may guess; first of all the ogre, and then all his kith and kin. But Shortshanks had brewed the wort so strong that they all fell down dead, one after another, like so many flies, as soon as they had tasted it. At last there wasn't one of them left alive but one vile old hag, who lay bedridden in the chimney-corner.

'Oh you poor old wretch,' said Shortshanks, 'you may just as well taste the wort along with the rest.'

So, he went and scooped up a little from the bottom of the copper in a scoop, and gave her a drink, and so he was rid of the whole pack of them.

As he stood there and looked about him, he cast his eye on a great chest, so he took it and filled it with gold and silver. Then he tied the cable round himself and the princess and the chest, and gave it a good tug, and his men pulled them all up, safe and sound. As soon as ever Shortshanks was well up, he said to the ship, 'Off and away, over fresh water and salt water, high hill and deep dale, and don't stop till you come to the king's palace.' And straightway the ship held on her course, so that the yellow billows foamed round her. When the people in the palace saw the ship sailing up, they were not slow in meeting them with songs and music, welcoming Shortshanks with great joy; but the gladdest of all was the king, who had now got his other daughter back again.

But now Shortshanks was rather down-hearted, for you must know that both the princesses wanted to have him, and he would have no other than the one he had first saved, and she was the youngest. So he walked up and down, and thought and thought what he should do to get her, and yet do something to please her sister. Well, one day as he was turning the thing over in his mind, it struck him if he only had his brother King Sturdy, who was so like him that no one could tell the one from the other. He would give up to him the other princess and half the kingdom, for he thought one-half was quite enough.

Well, as soon as ever this came into his mind, he went outside the palace and called on King Sturdy, but no one came. So he called a second time a little louder, but still no one came. Then he called out the third time 'King Sturdy' with all his might, and there stood his brother before him. 'Didn't I say!' he said to Shortshanks, 'didn't I say you were not to call me except in your utmost need? And here there is not so much as a gnat to do you any harm!' And with that he gave him such a box on the ear that Shortshanks tumbled head over heels on the grass.

'Now shame on you to hit so hard!' said Shortshanks. 'First of all I won a princess and half the kingdom, and then I won another princess and the other half of the kingdom; and now I'm thinking to give you one of the princesses and half the kingdom. Is there any rhyme or reason in giving me such a box on the ear?'

When King Sturdy heard that, he begged his brother to forgive him, and they were soon as good friends as ever again.

'Now,' said Shortshanks, 'you know, we are so much alike, that no one can tell the one from the other; so just change clothes with me and go into the palace; then the princesses will think it is I that am coming in, and the one that kisses you first you shall have for your wife, and I will have the other for mine.'

And he said this because he knew well enough that the elder king's daughter was the stronger, and so he could very well guess how things would go. As for King Sturdy, he was willing enough, so he changed clothes with his brother and went into the palace. But when he came into the princesses' bower they thought it was Shortshanks, and both ran up to him to kiss him; but the elder, who was stronger and bigger, pushed her sister on one side, and threw her arms round King Sturdy's neck, and gave him a kiss. And so he got her for his wife, and Shortshanks got the younger princess. Then they made ready for the wedding, and you may fancy what a grand one it was, when I tell you that the fame of it was noised abroad over seven kingdoms.

GUDBRAND ON THE HILLSIDE

BY G. W. DASENT

Once on a time, there was a man whose name was Gudbrand; he had a farm which lay far, far away upon a hillside, and so they called him Gudbrand on the Hillside.

Now, you must know this man and his goodwife lived so happily together, and understood one another so well, that all the husband did the wife thought so well done there was nothing like it in the world, and she was always glad whatever he turned his hand to. The farm was their own land, and they had a hundred dollars lying at the bottom of their chest, and two cows tethered up in a stall in their farmyard.

So one day his wife said to Gudbrand: 'Do you know, dear, I think we ought to take one of our cows into town, and sell it; that's what I think; for then we shall have some money in hand, and such well-to-do people as we ought to have ready money like the rest of the world. As for the hundred dollars at the bottom of the chest yonder, we can't make a hole in them, and I'm sure I don't know what we want with more than one cow. Besides, we shall gain a little in another way, for then I shall get off with only looking after one cow, instead of having, as now, to feed and litter and water two.'

Well, Gudbrand thought his wife talked right good sense, so he set off at once with the cow on his way to town to sell her, but when he got to the town, there was no one who would buy his cow.

'Well, well, never mind,' said Gudbrand, 'at the worst, I can only go back home again with my cow. I've both stable and tether for her, I should think, and the road is no farther out than in'; and with that he began to toddle home with his cow.

But when he had gone a bit of the way, a man met him who had a horse to sell, so Gudbrand thought 'twas better to have a horse than a cow, so he swopped with the man. A little farther on he met a man walking along and driving a fat pig before him, and he thought it better to have a fat pig than a horse, so he swopped with the man. After that he went a little farther, and a man met him with a goat, so he thought it better to have a goat than a pig, and he swopped with the man that owned the goat. Then he went on a good bit till he met a man who had a sheep, and he swopped with him too, for he thought it always better to have a sheep than a goat. After a while he met a man with a goose, and he swopped away the sheep for the goose; and when he had walked a long, long time, he met a man with a cock, and he swopped with him, for he thought in this wise, ''Tis surely better to have a cock than a goose.' Then he went on till the day was far spent, and he began to get very hungry, so he sold the cock for a shilling, and bought food with the money, for, thought Gudbrand on the Hillside, ''Tis always better to save one's life than to have a cock.'

After that he went on home till he reached his nearest neighbour's house, where he turned in.

'Well,' said the owner of the house, 'how did things go with you in town?'

'Rather so so,' said Gudbrand, 'I can't praise my luck, nor do I blame it either,' and with that he told the whole story from first to last.

'Ah!' said his friend, 'you'll get nicely called over the coals, that one can see, when you get home to your wife. Heaven help you, I wouldn't stand in your shoes for something.'

'Well,' said Gudbrand on the Hillside, 'I think things might have gone much worse with me; but now, whether I have done wrong or not, I have so kind a goodwife, she never has a word to say against anything that I do.'

'Oh,' answered his neighbour, 'I hear what you say, but I don't believe it for all that.'

'Shall we lay a bet upon it?' asked Gudbrand on the Hillside. 'I have a hundred dollars at the bottom of my chest at home; will you lay as many against them?'

Yes, the friend was ready to bet; so Gudbrand stayed there till evening, when it began to get dark, and then they went together to his house, and the neighbour was to stand outside the door and listen, while the man went in to see his wife.

'Good evening!' said Gudbrand on the Hillside.

'Good evening!' said the goodwife. 'Oh, is that you? Now God be praised.'

Yes, it was he. So the wife asked how things had gone with him in town?

'Oh, only so so,' answered Gudbrand, 'not much to brag of. When I got to the town there was no one who would buy the cow, so you must know I swopped it away for a horse.'

'For a horse,' said his wife. 'Well that is good of you. Thanks with all my heart. We are so well to do that we may drive to church, just as well as other people; and if we choose to keep a horse we have a right to get one, I should think. So run out, child, and put up the horse.'

'Ah!' said Gudbrand, 'but you see I've not got the horse after all; for when I got a bit farther on the road, I swopped it away for a pig.'

'Think of that, now!' said the wife. 'You did just as I should have done myself; a thousand thanks! Now I can have a bit of bacon in the house to set before people when they come to see me, that I can. What do we want with a horse? People would only say we had got so proud that we couldn't walk to church. Go out, child, and put up the pig in the sty.'

'But I've not got the pig either,' said Gudbrand, 'for when I got a little farther on, I swopped it away for a milch goat.'

'Bless us!' cried his wife, 'how well you manage everything! Now I think it over, what should I do with a pig? People would only point at us and say, "Yonder they eat up all they have got." No! Now I have got a goat, and I shall have milk and cheese, and keep the goat too. Run out, child, and put up the goat.'

'Nay, but I haven't got the goat either,' said Gudbrand, 'for a little farther on I swopped it away, and got a fine sheep instead.'

'You don't say so!' cried his wife. 'Why, you do everything to please me, just as if I had been with you. What do we want with a goat? If I had it I should lose half my time in climbing up the hills to get it down. No, if I have a sheep, I shall have both wool and clothing, and fresh meat in the house. Run out, child, and put up the sheep.'

'But I haven't got the sheep any more than the rest,' said Gudbrand; 'for when I had gone a bit farther, I swopped it away for a goose.'

'Thank you, thank you, with all my heart,' cried his wife. 'What should I do with a sheep? I have no spinning wheel, nor carding comb, nor should I care to worry myself with cutting, and shaping, and sewing clothes. We can buy clothes now, as we have always done, and now I shall have roast goose, which I have longed for so often, and, besides, down to stuff my little pillow with. Run out, child, and put up the goose.'

'Ah!' said Gudbrand, 'but I haven't the goose either, for when I had gone a bit farther I swopped it away for a cock.'

'Dear me!' cried his wife, 'how you think of everything! Just as I should have done myself. A cock! Think of that! Why it's as good as an eight-day clock, for every morning the cock crows at four o'clock, and we shall be able to stir our stumps in good time. What should we do with a goose? I don't know how to cook it; and as for my pillow, I can stuff it with cotton-grass. Run out, child, and put up the cock.'

'But, after all, I haven't got the cock,' said Gudbrand; 'for when I had gone a bit farther, I got as hungry as a hunter, so I was forced to sell the cock for a shilling, for fear I should starve.'

'Now, God be praised that you did so!' cried his wife. 'Whatever you do, you do it always just after my own heart. What should we do with the cock? We are our own masters, I should think, and can lie a-bed in the morning as long as we like. Heaven be thanked that I have got you safe back again; you who do everything so well that I want neither cock nor goose; neither pigs nor kine.'

Then Gudbrand opened the door and said, 'Well, what do you say now? Have I won the hundred dollars?' and his neighbour was forced to allow that he had.

THE LAD WHO WENT TO THE NORTH WIND

BY G. W. DASENT

Once on a time, there was an old widow who had one son. And as she was poorly and weak, her son had to go up into the safe to fetch meal for cooking, but when he got outside the safe, and was just going down the steps, there came the North Wind, puffing and blowing, caught up the meal, and so flew away with it through the air. Then the lad went back into the safe for more, but when he came out again on the steps, if the North Wind didn't come again and carry off the meal with a puff, and, more than that, he did so the third time. At this the lad got very angry, and as he thought it hard that the North Wind should behave so, he thought he'd just look him up, and ask him to give up his meal.

So off he went, but the way was long, and he walked and walked; but at last he came to the North Wind's house.

'Good day!' said the lad, 'and thank you for coming to see us yesterday.'

'GOOD DAY!' answered the North Wind, for his voice was loud and gruff, 'AND THANKS FOR COMING TO SEE ME. WHAT DO YOU WANT?'

'Oh!' answered the lad, 'I only wished to ask you to be so good as to let me have back that meal you took from me on the safe steps, for we haven't much to live on, and if you're to go on snapping up the morsel we have, there'll be nothing for it but to starve.'

'I haven't got your meal,' said the North Wind, 'but if you are in such need, I'll give you a cloth which will get you everything you want, if you only say, 'Cloth, spread yourself and serve up all kind of good dishes!'

With this the lad was well content. But, as the way was so long he couldn't get home in one day, so he turned into an inn on the way; and when they were going to sit down to supper he laid the cloth on a table which stood in the corner, and said, 'Cloth, spread yourself and serve up all kinds of good dishes.'

He had scarce said so before the cloth did as it was bid; and all who stood by thought it a fine thing, but most of all the landlady. So, when all were fast asleep at dead of night, she took the lad's cloth, and put another in its stead, just like the one he had got from the North Wind, but which couldn't so much as serve up a bit of dry bread.

So, when the lad woke, he took his cloth and went off with it, and that day he got home to his mother.

'Now,' said he, 'I've been to the North Wind's house, and a good fellow he is, for he gave me this cloth, and when I only say to it, "Cloth, spread yourself and serve up all kind of good dishes", I get any sort of food I please.'

'All very true, I daresay,' said his mother, 'but seeing is believing, and I shan't believe it till I see it.'

So the lad made haste, drew out a table, laid the cloth on it, and said, 'Cloth, spread yourself and serve up all kind of good dishes.' But never a bit of dry bread did the cloth serve up.

'Well,' said the lad, 'there's no help for it but to go to the North Wind again,' and away he went.

So he came to where the North Wind lived late in the afternoon.

'Good evening!' said the lad.

'Good evening!' said the North Wind.

'I want my rights for that meal of ours which you took,' said the lad, 'for, as for that cloth I got, it isn't worth a penny.'

'I've got no meal,' said the North Wind, 'but yonder you have a ram which coins nothing but golden ducats as soon as you say to it, "Ram, ram, make money!"'

So the lad thought this a fine thing, but as it was too far to get home that day, he turned in for the night to the same inn where he had slept before.

Before he called for anything, he tried the truth of what the North Wind had said of the ram, and found it all right, but, when the landlord saw that, he thought it was a famous ram, and, when the lad had fallen asleep, he took another which couldn't coin gold ducats, and changed the two.

Next morning off went the lad; and when he got home to his mother, he said: 'After all, the North Wind is a jolly fellow, for now he has given me a ram which can coin golden ducats if I only say "Ram, ram, make money".'

'All very true, I daresay,' said his mother, 'but I shan't believe any such stuff until I see the ducats made.'

'Ram, ram, make money!' said the lad, but if the ram made anything, it wasn't money.

So the lad went back again to the North Wind, and blew him up, and said the ram was worth nothing, and he must have his rights for the meal.

'Well!' said the North Wind, 'I've nothing else to give you but that old stick in the corner yonder, but it's a stick of that kind that if you say,'"Stick, stick, lay on!" it lays on till you say "Stick, stick, now stop!"'

So, as the way was long, the lad turned in this night too to the landlord, but as he could pretty well guess how things stood as to the cloth and the ram, he lay down at once on the bench and began to snore, as if he were asleep.

Now the landlord, who easily saw that the stick must be worth something, hunted up one which was like it, and when he heard the lad snore, was going to change the two, but, just as the landlord was about to take it, the lad bawled out, 'Stick, stick, lay on!'

So the stick began to beat the landlord, till he jumped over chairs, and tables, and benches, and yelled and roared:

'Oh my! oh my! Bid the stick be still, else it will beat me to death, and you shall have back both your cloth and your ram.'

When the lad thought the landlord had got enough, he said, 'Stick, stick, now stop!'

Then he took the cloth and put it into his pocket, and went home with his stick in his hand, leading the ram by a cord round its horns; and so he got his rights for the meal he had lost.

THE MASTER THIEF

BY G. W. DASENT

Once upon a time, there was a poor cottager who had three sons. He had nothing to leave them when he died, and no money with which to put them to any trade, so that he did not know what to make of them. At last he said he would give them leave to take to anything each liked best, and to go whithersoever they pleased, and he would go with them a bit of the way; and so he did. He went with them till they came to a place where three roads met, and there each of them chose a road, and their father bade them goodbye, and went back home. I have never heard tell what became of the two elder; but as for the youngest, he went both far and long, as you shall hear.

So it fell out one night as he was going through a great wood that such bad weather overtook him. It blew, and sleeted, and drove so that he could scarce keep his eyes open; and in a trice, before he knew how it was, he got bewildered, and could not find either road or path. But as he went on and on, at last he saw a glimmering of light far, far off in the wood. So he thought he would try to get to the light; and after a time he did reach it. There it was in a large house, and the fire was blazing so brightly inside, that he could tell the folk had not yet gone to bed; so he went in and saw an old dame bustling about and minding the house.

'Good evening!' said the youth.

'Good evening!' said the old dame.

'Hutetu! It's such foul weather out of doors tonight,' said he.

'So it is,' said she.

'Can I get leave to have a bed and shelter here tonight?' asked the youth.

'You'll get no good by sleeping here,' said the old dame, 'for if the folk come home and find you here, they'll kill both me and you.'

'What sort of folk, then, are they who live here?' asked the youth.

'Oh, robbers! And a bad lot of them too,' said the old dame. 'They stole me away when I was little, and have kept me as their housekeeper ever since.'

'Well, for all that, I think I'll just go to bed,' said the youth. 'Come what may, I'll not stir out at night in such weather.'

'Very well,' said the old dame. 'But if you stay, it will be the worse for you.'

With that the youth got into a bed which stood there, but he dared not go to sleep, and very soon after in came the robbers. So the old dame told them how a stranger fellow had come in whom she had not been able to get out of the house again.

'Did you see if he had any money?' asked the robbers.

'Such a one as he have money!' said the old dame, 'the tramper! Why, if he had clothes to his back, it was as much as he had.'

Then the robbers began to talk among themselves what they should do with him; if they should kill him outright, or what else they should do. Meantime the youth got up and began to talk to them, and to ask if they didn't want a servant, for it might be that he would be glad to enter their service.

'Oh,' said they. 'If you have a mind to follow the trade that we follow, you can very well get a place here.'

'It's all one to me what trade I follow,' said the youth, 'for when I left home, father gave me leave to take to any trade I chose.'

'Well, have you a mind to steal?' asked the robbers.

'I don't care',,said the youth, for he thought it would not take long to learn that trade.

Now there lived a man a little way off who had three oxen. One of these he was to take to the town to sell, and the robbers had heard what he was going to do, so they said to the youth, if he were good to steal the ox from the man by the way without his knowing it, and without doing him any harm, they would give him leave to be their serving-man.

Well, the youth set off, and took with him a pretty shoe, with a silver buckle on it, which lay about the house; and he put the shoe in the road along which the man was going with his ox; and when he had done that, he went into the wood and hid himself under a bush. So when the man came by he saw the shoe at once.

'That's a nice shoe,' said he. 'If I only had the fellow to it, I'd take it home with me, and perhaps I'd put my old dame in a good humour for once.' For you must know he had an old wife, so cross and snappish, it was not long between each time that she boxed his ears. But then he bethought him that he could do nothing with the odd shoe unless he had the fellow to it, so he went on his way and let the shoe lie on the road.

Then the youth took up the shoe, and made all the haste he could to get before the man by a short cut through the wood, and laid it down before him in the road again. When the man came along with his ox, he got quite angry with himself for being so dull as to leave the fellow to the shoe lying in the road instead of taking it with him; so he tied the ox to the fence, and said to himself, ‘I may just as well run back and pick up the other, and then I’ll have a pair of good shoes for my old dame, and so, perhaps, I’ll get a kind word from her for once.’

So he set off, and hunted and hunted up and down for the shoe, but no shoe did he find, and at length he had to go back with the one he had. But, meanwhile, the youth had taken the ox and gone off with it. And when the man came and saw his ox gone, he began to cry and bewail, for he was afraid his old dame would kill him outright when she came to know that the ox was lost. But just then it came across his mind that he would go home and take the second ox, and drive it to the town, and not let his old dame know anything about the matter. So he did this, and went home and took the ox without his dame’s knowing it, and set off with it to the town. But the robbers knew all about it, and they said to the youth, if he could get this ox too, without the man’s knowing it, and without his doing him any harm, he should be as good as anyone of them. If that were all, the youth said, he did not think it a very hard thing.

This time he took with him a rope, and hung himself up under the armpits to a tree right in the man’s way. So the man came along with his ox, and when he saw such a sight hanging there he began to feel a little queer.

‘Well,’ said he, ‘whatever heavy thoughts you had who have hanged yourself up there, it can’t be helped; you may hang for what I care! I can’t breathe life into you again.’ And with that he went on his way with his ox. Down slipped the youth from the tree, and ran by a footpath, and got before the man, and hung himself up right in his way again.

‘Bless me!’ said the man. ‘Were you really so heavy at heart that you hanged yourself up there – or is it only a piece of witchcraft that I see before me? Aye, aye, you may hang for all I care, whether you are a ghost or whatever you are!' So he passed on with his ox.

Now the youth did just as he had done twice before; he jumped down from the tree, ran through the wood by a footpath, and hung himself up right in the man's way again. But when the man saw this sight for the third time, he said to himself:

'Well! this is an ugly business! Is it likely now that they should have been so heavy at heart as to hang themselves, all these three? No, I cannot think it is anything else than a piece of witchcraft that I see. But now I'll soon know for certain; if the other two are still hanging there, it must be really so, but if they are not, then it can be nothing but witchcraft that I see.'

So he tied up his ox, and ran back to see if the others were still really hanging there. But while he went and peered up into all the trees, the youth jumped down and took his ox and ran off with it. When the man came back and found his ox gone, he was in a sad plight, and, as anyone might know without being told, he began to cry and bemoan; but at last he came to take it easier, and so he thought, 'There's no other help for it than to go home and take the third ox without my dame's knowing it, and to try and drive a good bargain with it, so that I may get a good sum of money for it.'

So he went home and set off with the ox, and his old dame knew never a word about the matter. But the robbers, they knew all about it, and they said to the youth, that if he could steal this ox as he had stolen the other two, then he should be master over the whole band. Well, the youth set off, and ran into the wood, and as the man came by with his ox he set up a dreadful bellowing, just like a great ox in the wood. When the man heard that, you can't think how glad he was, for it seemed to him that he knew the voice of his big bullock, and he thought that now he should find both of them again; so he tied up the third ox, and ran off from the road to look for them in the wood; but meantime the youth went off with the third ox. Now, when the man came back and found he had lost this ox too, he was so wild that there was no end to his grief. He cried and roared and beat his breast, and, to tell the truth, it was many days before he dared go home, for he was afraid lest his old dame should kill him outright on the spot.

As for the robbers, they were not very well pleased either, when they had to own that the youth was master over the whole band. So one day they thought they would try their hands at something which he was not man enough to do, and they set off all together, every man Jack of them, and left him alone at home. Now, the first thing that he did when they were all well clear of the house, was to drive the oxen out to the road, so that they might run back to the man from whom he had stolen them – and right glad he was to see them, as you may fancy. Next, he took all the horses which the robbers had, and loaded them with the best things he could lay his hands on – gold and silver, and clothes and other fine things – and then he bade the old dame to greet the robbers when they came back, and to thank them for him, and to say that now he was setting off on his travels, and they would have hard work to find him again; and with that, off he started.

After a good bit he came to the road along which he was going when he fell among the robbers, and when he got near home, and could see his father's cottage, he put on a uniform which he had found among the clothes he had taken from the robbers, and which was made just like a general's. So he drove up to the door as if he were any other great man. After that he went in and asked if he could have a lodging? No, that he couldn't at any price.

'How ever should I be able,' said the man, 'to make room in my house for such a fine gentleman – I who scarce have a rag to lie upon, and miserable rags too?'

'You always were a stingy old hunks,' said the youth, 'and so you are still, when you won't take your own son in.'

'What, you my son!' said the man.

'Don't you know me again?' said the youth. Well, after a little while he did know him again.

'But what have you been turning your hand to, that you have made yourself so great a man in such haste?' asked the man.

'Oh! I'll soon tell you,' said the youth. 'You said I might take to any trade I chose, and so I bound myself apprentice to a pack of thieves and robbers, and now I've served my time out, and am become a Master Thief.'

Now there lived a squire close by to his father's cottage, and he had such a great house, and such heaps of money, he could not tell how much he had. He had a daughter too, and a smart and pretty girl she was. So the Master Thief set his heart upon having her to wife, and he told his father to go to the squire and ask for his daughter for him.

'If he asks by what trade I get my living, you can say I'm a Master Thief.'

'I think you've lost your wits,' said the man, 'for you can't be in your right mind when you think of such stuff.'

No, he had not lost his wits. His father must and should go to the Squire, and ask for his daughter.

'Nay, but I tell you, I daren't go to the squire and be your spokesman; he who is so rich, and has so much money,' said the man.

Yes, there was no help for it, said the Master Thief – he should go whether he would or no – and if he did not go by fair means, he would soon make him go by foul. But the man was still loath to go, so he stepped after him, and rubbed him down with a good birch cudgel, and kept on till the man came crying and sobbing inside the squire's door.

'How now, my man! What ails you?' asked the squire. So he told him the whole story: how he had three sons who set off one day, and how he had given them leave to go whithersoever they would, and to follow whatever calling they chose. 'And here now is the youngest come home, and has thrashed me till he has made me come to you and ask for your daughter for him to wife; and he bids me say, besides, that he's a Master Thief.' And so he fell to crying and sobbing again.

'Never mind, my man,' said the squire, laughing. 'Just go back and tell him from me, he must prove his skill first. If he can steal the roast from the spit in the kitchen on Sunday, while all the household are looking after it, he shall have my daughter. Just go and tell him that.'

So he went back and told the youth, who thought it would be an easy job. So he set about and caught three hares alive, and put them into a bag, and dressed himself in some old rags, until he looked so poor and filthy that it made one's heart bleed to see; and then he stole into the passage at the back door of the squire's house on the Sunday forenoon, with his bag, just like any other beggar boy. But the squire himself and all his household were in the kitchen watching the roast. Just as they were doing this, the youth let one hare go, and it set off and ran round and round the yard in front of the house.

'Oh, just look at that hare!' said the folk in the kitchen, and were all for running out to catch it.

Yes, the squire saw it running too. 'Oh, let it run,' said he; 'there's no use in thinking to catch a hare on the spring.'

A little while after, the youth let the second hare go, and they saw it in the kitchen, and thought it was the same they had seen before, and still wanted to run out and catch it; but the squire said again it was no use. It was not long before the youth let the third hare go, and it set off and ran round and round the yard as the others before it. Now they saw it from the kitchen, and still thought it was the same hare that kept on running about, and were all eager to be out after it.

'Well, it is a fine hare,' said the squire. 'Come, let's see if we can't lay our hands on it.'

So out he ran, and the rest with him – away they all went, the hare before, and they after – so that it was rare fun to see. But meantime the youth took the roast and ran off with it. And where the squire got a roast for his dinner that day I don't know, but one thing I know, and that is, that he had no roast hare, though he ran after it till he was both warm and weary.

Now it chanced that the priest came to dinner that day, and when the squire told him what a trick the Master Thief had played him, he made such game of him that there was no end of it. 'For my part,' said the priest, 'I can't think how it could ever happen to me to be made such a fool of by a fellow like that.'

'Very well – only keep a sharp look-out,' said the squire. 'Maybe he'll come to see you before you know a word of it.' But the priest stuck to his text – that he did, and made game of the squire because he had been so taken in.

Later in the afternoon came the Master Thief, and wanted to have the squire's daughter, as he had given his word. But the squire began to talk him over, and said, 'Oh, you must first prove your skill a little more; for what you did today was no great thing, after all. Couldn't you now play off a good trick on the priest, who is sitting in there, and making game of me for letting such a fellow as you twist me round his thumb?'

'Well, as for that, it wouldn't be hard,' said the Master Thief. So he dressed himself up like a bird, threw a great white sheet over his body, took the wings of a goose and tied them to his back, and so climbed up into a great maple which stood in the priest's garden. And when the priest came home in the evening, the youth began to bawl out, 'Father Laurence! Father Laurence!' – for that was the priest's name.

'Who is that calling me?' said the priest.

'I am an angel,' said the Master Thief, 'sent from God to let you know that you shall be taken up alive into heaven for your piety's sake. Next Monday night you must hold yourself ready for the journey, for I shall come then to fetch you in a sack, and all your gold and your silver, and all that you have of this world's goods, you must lay together in a heap in your dining room.'

Well, Father Laurence fell on his knees before the angel, and thanked him; and the very next day he preached a farewell sermon, and gave it out how there had come down an angel unto the big maple in his garden, who had told him that he was to be taken up alive into heaven for his piety's sake; and he preached and made such a touching discourse, that all who were at church wept, both young and old.

So the next Monday night came the Master Thief like an angel again, and the priest fell on his knees and thanked him before he was put into the sack; but when he had got him well in, the Master Thief drew and dragged him over stocks and stones.

'OW! OW!' groaned the priest inside the sack, 'wherever are we going?'

'This is the narrow way which leadeth unto the kingdom of heaven,' said the Master Thief, who went on dragging him along till he had nearly broken every bone in his body. At last he tumbled him into a goose-house that belonged to the squire, and the geese began pecking and pinching him with their bills, so that he was more dead than alive.

'Now you are in the flames of purgatory, to be cleansed and purified for life everlasting,' said the Master Thief; and with that he went his way, and took all the gold which the priest had laid together in his dining room. The next morning, when the goose-girl came to let the geese out, she heard how the priest lay in the sack, and bemoaned himself in the goose-house.

'In heaven's name, who's there, and what ails you?' she cried.

'Oh!' said the priest, 'if you are an angel from heaven, do let me out, and let me return again to earth, for it is worse here than in hell. The little fiends keep on pinching me with tongs.'

'Heaven help us, I am no angel at all,' said the girl, as she helped the priest out of the sack. 'I only look after the squire's geese, and like enough they are the little fiends which have pinched your reverence.'

'Oh!' groaned the priest, 'this is all that Master Thief's doing. Ah, my gold and my silver, and my fine clothes!' And he beat his breast, and hobbled home at such a rate that the girl thought he had lost his wits all at once.

Now when the squire came to hear how it had gone with the priest, and how he had been along the narrow way, and into purgatory, he laughed till he well-nigh split his sides. But when the Master Thief came and asked for his daughter as he had promised, the squire put him off again, and said:

'You must do one masterpiece better still, that I may see plainly what you are fit for. Now, I have twelve horses in my stable, and on them I will put twelve grooms, one on each. If you are so good a thief as to steal the horses from under them, I'll see what I can do for you.'

'Very well, I daresay I can do it,' said the Master Thief, 'but shall I really have your daughter if I can?'

'Yes, if you can, I'll do my best for you,' said the squire. So the Master Thief set off to a shop, and bought brandy enough to fill two pocket flasks, and into one of them he put a sleepy drink, but into the other only brandy. After that he hired eleven men to lie in wait at night, behind the squire's stable yard; and last of all, for fair words and a good bit of money, he borrowed a ragged gown and cloak from an old woman; and so, with a staff in his hand, and a bundle at his back, he limped off, as evening drew on, towards the squire's stable. Just as he got there they were watering the horses for the night, and had their hands full of work. 'What the devil do you want?' said one of the grooms to the old woman.

'Oh, oh! hutetu! It is so bitter cold,' said she, and shivered and shook, and made wry faces. 'Hutetu! It is so cold, a poor wretch may easily freeze to death.' And with that she fell to shivering and shaking again.

'Oh, for the love of heaven! Can I get leave to stay here a while, and sit inside the stable door?'

'To the devil with your leave,' said one. 'Pack yourself off this minute, for if the squire sets his eye on you, he'll lead us a pretty dance.'

'Oh, the poor old bag-of-bones!' said another, whose heart took pity on her, 'the old hag may sit inside and welcome; such a one as she can do no harm.'

And the rest said, some she should stay, and some she shouldn't; but while they were quarrelling and minding the horses, she crept further and further into the stable, till at last she sat herself down behind the door; and when she had got so far, no one gave any more heed to her.

As the night wore on, the men found it rather cold work to sit so still and quiet on horseback.

'Hutetu! It is so devilish cold,' said one, and beat his arms crosswise.

'That it is,' said another. 'I freeze so, that my teeth chatter.'

'If one only had a quid to chew,' said a third.

Well, there was one who had an ounce or two; so they shared it between them, though it wasn't much, after all, that each got; and so they chewed and spat, and spat and chewed. This helped them somewhat, but in a little while they were just as bad as ever.

'Hutetu!' said one, and shivered and shook.

'Hutetu!' said the old woman, and shivered so, that every tooth in her head chattered. Then she pulled out the flask with brandy in it, and her hand shook so that the spirit splashed about in the flask, and then she took such a gulp, that it went 'bop' in her throat.

'What's that you've got in your flask, old girl?' asked one of the grooms.

'Oh, it's only a drop of brandy, old man,' said she.

'Brandy! Well, I never! Do let me have a drop,' screamed the whole twelve, one after another.

'Oh, but it is such a little drop,' mumbled the old woman, 'it will not even wet your mouths round.' But they must and would have it – there was no help for it – and so she pulled out the flask with the sleepy drink in it, and put it to the first man's lips; then she shook no more, but guided the flask so that each of them got what he wanted, and the twelfth had not done drinking before the first sat and snored. Then the Master Thief threw off his beggar's rags and took one groom after the other so softly off their horses, and set them astride on the beams between the stalls; and so he called his eleven men, and rode off with the squire's twelve horses. But when the squire got up in the morning, and went to look after his grooms, they had just begun to come to; and some of them fell to spurring the beams with their spurs, till the splinters flew again, and some fell off, and some still hung on and sat there looking like fools.

'Ho! ho!' said the squire. 'I see very well who has been here; but as for you, a pretty set of blockheads you must be to sit here and let the Master Thief steal the horses from between your legs.'

So they all got a good leathering because they had not kept a sharper look-out.

Further on in the day came the Master Thief again, and told how he had managed the matter, and asked for the squire's daughter, as he had promised; but the squire gave him one hundred dollars down, and said he must do something better still.

'Do you think now,' said he, 'you can steal the horse from under me while I am out riding on his back?'

'Oh, yes! I daresay I could,' said the Master Thief, 'if I were really sure of getting your daughter.'

Well, well, the squire would see what he could do; and he told the Master Thief a day when he would be taking a ride on a great common where they drilled the troops. So the Master Thief soon got hold of an old worn-out jade of a mare, and set to work, and made traces and collar of withies and broom-twigs, and bought an old beggarly cart and a great cask. After that he told an old beggar woman, he would give her ten dollars if she would get inside the cask, and keep her mouth agape over the taphole, into which he was going to stick his finger. No harm should happen to her; she should only be driven about a little; and if he took his finger out more than once, she was to have ten dollars more. Then he threw a few rags and tatters over himself, and stuffed himself out, and put on a wig and a great beard of goat's hair, so that no one could know him again, and set off for the common, where the squire had already been riding about a good bit. When he reached the place, he went along so softly and slowly that he scarce made an inch of way. 'Gee up! Gee up!' and so he went on a little; then he stood stock still, and so on a little again; and altogether the pace was so poor it never once came into the squire's head that this could be the Master Thief.

At last the squire rode right up to him, and asked if he had seen anyone lurking about in the wood thereabouts. 'No,' said the man, 'I haven't seen a soul.'

'Harkye, now,' said the squire, 'if you have a mind to ride into the wood, and hunt about and see if you can fall upon anyone lurking about there, you shall have the loan of my horse, and a shilling into the bargain, to drink my health, for your pains.'

'I don't see how I can go,' said the man, 'for I am going to a wedding with this cask of mead, which I have been to town to fetch, and here the tap has fallen out by the way, and so I must go along, holding my finger in the taphole.'

'Ride off,' said the squire. 'I'll look after your horse and cask.'

Well, on these terms the man was willing to go; but he begged the Squire to be quick in putting his finger into the taphole when he took his own out, and to mind and keep it there till he came back. At last the squire grew weary of standing there with his finger in the taphole, so he took it out.

'Now I shall have ten dollars more!' screamed the old woman inside the cask. And then the squire saw at once how the land lay, and took himself off home; but he had not gone far before they met him with a fresh horse, for the Master Thief had already been to his house, and told them to send one. The day after, he came to the squire and would have his daughter, as he had given his word; but the squire put him off again with fine words, and gave him two hundred dollars, and said he must do one more masterpiece. If he could do that, he should have her. Well, well, the Master Thief thought he could do it, if he only knew what it was to be.

'Do you think, now,' said the squire, 'you can steal the sheet off our bed, and the shift off my wife's back. Do you think you could do that?'

'It shall be done,' said the Master Thief. 'I only wish I was as sure of getting your daughter.'

So when night began to fall, the Master Thief went out and cut down a thief who hung on the gallows, and threw him across his shoulders, and carried him off. Then he got a long ladder and set it up against the squire's bedroom window, and so climbed up, and kept bobbing the dead man up and down, just for all the world like one that was peeping in at the window.

'That's the Master Thief, old lass!' said the squire, and gave his wife a nudge on the side. 'Now see if I don't shoot him, that's all.'

So saying he took up a rifle which he had laid at his bedside.

'No! no! pray don't shoot him after telling him he might come and try,' said his wife.

'Don't talk to me, for shoot him I will,' said he; and so he lay there and aimed and aimed, but as soon as the head came up before the window, and he saw a little of it, so soon was it down again. At last he thought he had a good aim: 'bang' went the gun, down fell the dead body to the ground with a heavy thump, and down went the Master Thief too as fast as he could.

'Well,' said the squire, 'it is quite true that I am the chief magistrate in these parts, but people are fond of talking, and it would be a bore if they came to see this dead man's body. I think the best thing to be done is that I should go down and bury him.'

'You must do as you think best, dear,' said his wife. So the squire got out of bed and went downstairs, and he had scarce put his foot out of the door before the Master Thief stole in, and went straight upstairs to his wife.

'Why, dear, back already!' said she, for she thought it was her husband.

'O yes, I only just put him into a hole, and threw a little earth over him. It is enough that he is out of sight, for it is such a bad night out of doors; by-and-by I'll do it better. But just let me have the sheet to wipe myself with – he was so bloody – and I have made myself in such a mess with him.'

So he got the sheet.

After a while he said, 'Do you know I am afraid you must let me have your nightshift too, for the sheet won't do by itself, that I can see.'

So she gave him the shift also. But just then it came across his mind that he had forgotten to lock the house door, so he must step down and look to that before he came back to bed, and away he went with both shift and sheet.

A little while after came the true squire.

'Why, what a time you've taken to lock the door, dear!' said his wife. 'And what have you done with the sheet and shift?'

'What do you say?' said the squire.

'Why, I am asking what you have done with the sheet and shift that you had to wipe off the blood,' said she.

'What, in the Devil's name!' said the squire. 'Has he taken me in this time too?'

Next day came the Master Thief and asked for the squire's daughter, as he had given his word; and then the squire dared not do anything else than give her to him, and a good lump of money into the bargain; for, to tell the truth, he was afraid lest the Master Thief should steal the eyes out of his head, and that the people would begin to say spiteful things of him if he broke his word. So the Master Thief lived well and happily from that time forward. I don't know whether he stole any more, but if he did, I am quite sure it was only for the sake of a bit of fun.

THE THREE BILLY-GOATS GRUFF

BY G. W. DASENT

Once on a time, there were three billy-goats, who were to go up to the hillside to make themselves fat, and the name of all three was 'Gruff'.

On the way up was a bridge over a burn they had to cross, and under the bridge lived a great ugly troll, with eyes as big as saucers, and a nose as long as a poker.

So first of all came the youngest billy-goat Gruff to cross the bridge.

'Trip, trap; trip, trap!' went the bridge.

'WHO'S THAT tripping over my bridge?' roared the troll.

'Oh, it is only I, the tiniest billy-goat Gruff, and I'm going up to the hillside to make myself fat,' said the billy-goat, with such a small voice.

'Now, I'm coming to gobble you up,' said the troll.

'Oh, no, pray don't take me! I'm too little, that I am,' said the billy-goat. 'Wait a bit till the second billy-goat Gruff comes – he's much bigger.'

'Well, be off with you,' said the troll.

A little while after came the second billy-goat Gruff to cross the bridge.

'Trip, trap; trip, trap; trip, trap!' went the bridge.

'WHO'S THAT tripping over my bridge?' roared the troll.

'Oh, it's the second billy-goat Gruff, and I'm going up to the hillside to make myself fat,' said the billy-goat, who hadn't such a small voice.

'Now, I'm coming to gobble you up,' said the troll.

'Oh, no, don't take me! Wait a little till the big billy-goat Gruff comes – he's much bigger.'

'Very well, be off with you,' said the troll.

But just then up came the big billy-goat Gruff.

'TRIP, TRAP! TRIP, TRAP! TRIP, TRAP!' went the bridge, for the billy-goat was so heavy that the bridge creaked and groaned under him.

'WHO'S THAT tramping over my bridge?' roared the troll.

'IT'S I! THE BIG BILLY-GOAT GRUFF,' said the billy-goat, who had an ugly hoarse voice of his own.

'Now, I'm coming to gobble you up,' roared the troll.

Well, come along! I've got two spears,
And I'll poke your eyeballs out at your ears;
I've got besides two curling-stones,
And I'll crush you to bits, body and bones.

That was what the big billy-goat said; and so he flew at the troll and poked his eyes out with his horns, and crushed him to bits, body and bones, and tossed him out into the burn, and after that he went up to the hillside. There the billy-goats got so fat they were scarce able to walk home again; and if the fat hasn't fallen off them, why they're still fat; and so:

Snip, snap, snout,
This tale's told out.

DAPPLEGRIM

BY G. W. DASENT

Once on a time, there was a rich couple who had twelve sons; but the youngest when he was grown up, said he wouldn't stay any longer at home, but be off into the world to try his luck. His father and mother said he did very well at home, and had better stay where he was. But no, he couldn't rest; away he must and would go. So at last they gave him leave. And when he had walked a good bit, he came to a king's palace, where he asked for a place, and got it.

Now the daughter of the king of that land had been carried off into the hill by a troll, and the king had no other children; so he and all his land were in great grief and sorrow, and the king gave his word that anyone who could set her free should have the princess and half the kingdom. But there was no one who could do it, though many tried.

So when the lad had been there a year or so, he longed to go home again and see his father and mother, and back he went, but when he got home his father and mother were dead, and his brothers had shared all that the old people owned between them, and so there was nothing left for the lad.

'Shan't I have anything at all, then, out of father's and mother's goods?' asked the lad.

'Who could tell you were still alive, when you went gadding and wandering about so long?' said his brothers. 'But all the same, there are twelve mares up on the hill which we haven't yet shared among us; if you choose to take them for your share, you're quite welcome.'

Yes, the lad was quite content; so he thanked his brothers, and went at once up on the hill, where the twelve mares were out at grass. And when he got up there and found them, each of them had a foal at her side, and one of them had besides, along with her, a big dapple-grey foal, which was so sleek that the sun shone from its coat.

'A fine fellow you are, my little foal,' said the lad.

'Yes,' said the foal. 'But if you'll only kill all the other foals, so that I may run and suck all the mares one year more, you'll see how big and sleek I'll be then.'

Yes, the lad was ready to do that; so he killed all those twelve foals and went home again.

So when he came back the next year to look after his foal and mares, the foal was so fat and sleek that the sun shone from its coat, and it had grown so big, the lad had hard work to mount it. As for the mares, they had each of them another foal.

'Well, it's quite plain I lost nothing by letting you suck all my twelve mares,' said the lad to the yearling, 'but now you're big enough to come along with me.'

'No,' said the colt, 'I must bide here a year longer. And now kill all the twelve foals that I may suck all the mares this year too, and you'll see how big and sleek I'll be by summer.'

Yes, the lad did that; and next year when he went up on the hill to look after his colt and the mares, each mare had her foal, but the dapple colt was so tall the lad couldn't reach up to his crest when he wanted to feel how fat he was; and so sleek he was too, that his coat glistened in the sunshine.

'Big and beautiful you were last year, my colt,' said the lad, 'but this year you're far grander. There's no such horse in the king's stable. But now you must come along with me.'

'No,' said Dapple again, 'I must stay here one year more. Kill the twelve foals as before that I may suck the mares the whole year, and then just come and look at me when the summer comes.'

Yes, the lad did that; he killed the foals, and went away home.

But when he went up next year to look after Dapple and the mares, he was quite astonished. So tall, and stout, and sturdy, he never thought a horse could be; for Dapple had to lie down on all fours before the lad could bestride him, and it was hard work to get up even then, although he lay flat; and his coat was so smooth and sleek, the sunbeams shone from it as from a looking-glass.

This time Dapple was willing enough to follow the lad, so he jumped up on his back, and when he came riding home to his brothers, they all clapped their hands and crossed themselves, for such a horse they had never heard of nor seen before.

'If you will only get me the best shoes you can for my horse, and the grandest saddle and bridle that are to be found,' said the lad, 'you may have my twelve mares that graze up on the hill yonder, and their twelve foals into the bargain.' For you must know that this year too every mare had her foal.

Yes, his brothers were ready to do that, and so the lad got such strong shoes under his horse that the stones flew high aloft as he rode away across the hills; and he had a golden saddle and a golden bridle, which gleamed and glistened a long way off.

'Now we're off to the king's palace,' said Dapplegrim – that was his name, 'but mind you ask the king for a good stable and good fodder for me.'

Yes, the lad said he would mind – he'd be sure not to forget – and when he rode off from his brothers' house, you may be sure it wasn't long, with such a horse under him, before he got to the king's palace.

When he came there the king was standing on the steps, and stared and stared at the man who came riding along.

'Nay, nay!' said he, 'such a man and such a horse I never yet saw in all my life.'

But when the lad asked if he could get a place in the king's household, the king was so glad he was ready to jump and dance as he stood on the steps.

Well, they said, perhaps he might get a place there.

'Aye,' said the lad, 'but I must have good stable-room for my horse, and fodder that one can trust.'

Yes, he should have meadow-hay and oats, as much as Dapple could cram, and all the other knights had to lead their horses out of the stable that Dapplegrim might stand alone, and have it all to himself.

But it wasn't long before all the others in the king's household began to be jealous of the lad, and there was no end to the bad things they would have done to him, if they had only dared. At last they thought of telling the king he had said he was man enough to set the king's daughter free – whom the Troll had long since carried away into the hill – if he only chose. The king called the lad before him, and said he had heard the lad said he was good to do so and so; so now he must go and do it. If he did it, he knew how the king had promised his daughter and half the kingdom, and that promise would be faithfully kept; if he didn't, he should be killed.

The lad kept on saying he never said any such thing, but it

was no good – the king wouldn't even listen to him; and so the end of it was he was forced to say he'd go and try.

So he went into the stable, down in the mouth and heavy-hearted, and then Dapplegrim asked him at once why he was in such dumps.

Then the lad told him all, and how he couldn't tell which way to turn:

'For as for setting the princess free, that's downright stuff.'

'Oh, but it might be done, perhaps,' said Dapplegrim. 'I'll help you through, but you must first have me well shod. You must go and ask for ten pounds of iron and twelve pounds of steel for the shoes, and one smith to hammer and another to hold.'

Yes, the lad did that, and got for answer 'Yes!' He got both the iron and the steel, and the smiths, and so Dapplegrim was shod both strong and well, and off went the lad from the court-yard in a cloud of dust.

But when he came to the hill into which the princess had been carried, the pinch was how to get up the steep wall of rock where the troll's cave was, in which the princess had been hid. For you must know the hill stood straight up and down right on end, as upright as a house wall, and as smooth as a sheet of glass.

The first time the lad went at it he got a little way up, but then Dapple's forelegs slipped, and down they went again, with a sound like thunder on the hill.

The second time he rode at it he got some way further up, but then one foreleg slipped, and down they went with a crash like a landslip.

But the third time Dapple said, 'Now we must show our mettle'; and went at it again till the stones flew heaven-high about them, and so they got up.

Then the lad rode right into the cave at full speed, and caught up the princess, and threw her over his saddle-bow and out and down again before the troll had time even to get on his legs; and so the princess was freed.

When the lad came back to the palace, the king was both happy and glad to get his daughter back – that you may well believe – but somehow or other, though I don't know how, the others about the court had so brought it about that the king was angry with the lad after all.

'Thanks you shall have for freeing my Princess,' said he to the lad, when he brought the princess into the hall, and made his bow.

'She ought to be mine as well as yours; for you're a word-fast man, I hope,' said the lad.

'Aye, aye!' said the king, 'have her you shall, since I said it; but first of all, you must make the sun shine into my palace hall.'

Now, you must know there was a high steep ridge of rock close outside the windows, which threw such a shade over the hall that never a sunbeam shone into it.

'That wasn't in our bargain,' answered the lad, 'but I see this is past praying against. I must e'en go and try my luck, for the princess I must and will have.'

So down he went to Dapple, and told him what the king wanted, and Dapplegrim thought it might easily be done, but first of all he must be new shod; and for that ten pounds of iron, and twelve pounds of steel besides, were needed, and two smiths, one to hammer and the other to hold, and then they'd soon get the sun to shine into the palace hall.

So when the lad asked for all these things, he got them at once – the king couldn't say nay for very shame – and so

Dapplegrim got new shoes, and such shoes! Then the lad jumped upon his back, and off they went again; and for every leap that Dapplegrim gave, down sank the ridge fifteen ells into the earth, and so they went on till there was nothing left of the ridge for the king to see.

When the lad got back to the king's palace, he asked the king if the Princess were not his now, for now no one could say that the sun didn't shine into the hall. But then the others set the king's back up again, and he answered the lad should have her, of course, he had never thought of anything else; but first of all he must get as grand a horse for the bride to ride on to church as the bridegroom had himself.

The lad said the king hadn't spoken a word about this before, and that he thought he had now fairly earned the princess, but the king held to his own, and more, if the lad couldn't do that he should lose his life – that was what the king said. So the lad went down to the stable in doleful dumps, as you may well fancy, and there he told Dapplegrim all about it; how the king had laid that task on him, to find the bride as good a horse as the bridegroom had himself, else he would lose his life.

'But that's not so easy,' he said, 'for your match isn't to be found in the wide world.'

'Oh yes, I have a match,' said Dapplegrim, 'but 'tisn't so easy to find him, for he abides in Hell. Still we'll try. And now you must go up to the king and ask for new shoes for me, ten pounds of iron, and twelve pounds of steel, and two smiths, one to hammer and one to hold – and mind you see that the points and ends of these shoes are sharp – and twelve sacks of rye, and twelve sacks of barley, and twelve slaughtered oxen, we must have with us; and mind, we must have the twelve ox-hides, with twelve hundred spikes driven into each; and, let me see, a big tar barrel – that's all we want.'

So the lad went up to the king and asked for all that Dapplegrim had said, and the king again thought he couldn't say nay, for shame's sake, and so the lad got all he wanted.

Well, he jumped up on Dapplegrim's back, and rode away from the palace, and when he had ridden far far over hill and heath, Dapple asked: 'Do you hear anything?'

'Yes, I hear an awful hissing and rustling up in the air,' said the lad. 'I think I'm getting afraid.'

'That's all the wild birds that fly through the wood. They are sent to stop us, but just cut a hole in the corn sacks, and then they'll have so much to do with the corn, they'll forget us quite.'

Yes, the lad did that; he cut holes in the corn sacks, so that the rye and barley ran out on all sides. Then all the wild birds that were in the wood came flying round them so thick that the sunbeams grew dark. But as soon as they saw the corn, they couldn't keep to their purpose, but flew down and began to pick and scratch at the rye and barley, and after that they began to fight among themselves. As for Dapplegrim and the lad, they forgot all about them, and did them no harm.

So the lad rode on and on – far, far over mountain and dale, over sand hills and moor. Then Dapplegrim began to prick up his ears again, and at last he asked the lad if he heard anything?

'Yes, now I hear such an ugly roaring and howling in the wood all round, it makes me quite afraid.'

'Ah!' said Dapplegrim, 'that's all the wild beasts that range through the wood, and they're sent out to stop us. But just cast out the twelve carcasses of the oxen – that will give them enough to do, and so they'll forget us outright.'

Yes, the lad cast out the carcasses, and then all the wild beasts in the wood, both bears, and wolves, and lions – all fell beasts of all kinds – came after them. But when they saw the carcasses, they began to fight for them among themselves till blood flowed in streams; but Dapplegrim and the lad they quite forgot.

So the lad rode far away, and they changed the landscape many, many times, for Dapplegrim didn't let the grass grow under him, as you may fancy. At last Dapple gave a great neigh.

'Do you hear anything?' he said.

'Yes, I hear something like a colt neighing loud, a long, long way off,' answered the lad.

'That's a full-grown colt then,' said Dapplegrim. 'If we hear him neigh so loud such a long way off.'

After that they travelled a good bit, changing the landscape once or twice, maybe. Then Dapplegrim gave another neigh.

'Now listen, and tell me if you hear anything,' he said.

'Yes, now I hear a neigh like a full-grown horse,' answered the lad.

'Aye, aye!' said Dapplegrim, 'you'll hear him once again soon, and then you'll hear he's got a voice of his own.'

So they travelled on and on, and changed the landscape once or twice, perhaps, and then Dapplegrim neighed the third time; but before he could ask the lad if he heard anything, something gave such a neigh across the heathy hillside, the lad thought hill and rock would surely be rent asunder.

'Now, he's here!' said Dapplegrim. 'Make haste, now, and throw the ox hides, with the spikes in them, over me, and throw down the tar barrel on the plain; then climb up into that great spruce fir yonder. When it comes, fire will flash out of both nostrils, and then the tar barrel will catch fire. Now, mind what

I say. If the flame rises, I win; if it falls, I lose; but if you see me winning take and cast the bridle – you must take it off me – over its head, and then it will be tame enough.'

So just as the lad had done throwing the ox hides with the spikes, over Dapplegrim, and had cast down the tar barrel on the plain, and had got well up into the spruce fir, up galloped a horse, with fire flashing out of his nostrils, and the flame caught the tar barrel at once. Then Dapplegrim and the strange horse began to fight till the stones flew heaven high. They fought and bit, and kicked, both with fore-feet and hind-feet, and sometimes the lad could see them, and sometimes he couldn't; but at last the flame began to rise, for wherever the strange horse kicked or bit, he met the spiked hides, and at last he had to yield. When the lad saw that, he wasn't long in getting down from the tree, and in throwing the bridle over its head, and then it was so tame you could hold it with a pack-thread.

And what do you think? That horse was dappled too, and so like Dapplegrim, you couldn't tell which was which. Then the lad bestrode the new Dapple he had broken, and rode home to the palace, and old Dapplegrim ran loose by his side. So when he got home, there stood the king out in the yard.

'Can you tell me now,' said the lad, 'which is the horse I have caught and broken, and which is the one I had before. If you can't, I think your daughter is fairly mine.'

Then the king went and looked at both Dapples, high and low, before and behind, but there wasn't a hair on one which wasn't on the other as well. 'No,' said the king, 'that I can't; and since you've got my daughter such a grand horse for her wedding, you shall have her with all my heart. But still, we'll have one trial more, just to see whether you're fated to have her. First, she shall hide herself twice, and then you shall hide yourself twice. If you can find out her hiding place, and she can't find out yours, why then you're fated to have her, and so you shall have her.'

'That's not in the bargain either,' said the lad, 'but we must just try, since it must be so.' And so the princess went off to hide herself first.

So she turned herself into a duck, and lay swimming on a pond that was close to the palace. But the lad only ran down to the stable and asked Dapplegrim what she had done with herself.

'Oh, you only need to take your gun,' said Dapplegrim, 'and go down to the brink of the pond, and aim at the duck which lies swimming about there, and she'll soon show herself.'

So the lad snatched up his gun and ran off to the pond. 'I'll just take a pop at this duck,' he said, and began to aim at it.

'Nay, nay, dear friend, don't shoot. It's I,' said the princess.

So he had found her once.

The second time the princess turned herself into a loaf of bread, and laid herself on the table among four other loaves; and so like was she to the others, no one could say which was which.

But the lad went again down to the stable to Dapplegrim, and said how the princess had hidden herself again, and he couldn't tell at all what had become of her.

'Oh, just take and sharpen a good bread knife,' said Dapplegrim, 'and do as if you were going to cut in two the third loaf on the left hand of those four loaves which are lying on the dresser in the king's kitchen, and you'll find her soon enough.'

Yes, the lad was down in the kitchen in no time, and began to sharpen the biggest bread knife he could lay hands on; then he caught hold of the third loaf on the left hand, and put the knife to it, as though he was going to cut it in two. 'I'll just have a slice off this loaf,' he said.

'Nay, dear friend,' said the princess, 'don't cut. It's I.' So he had found her twice.

Then he was to go and hide; but he and Dapplegrim had settled it all so well beforehand, it wasn't easy to find him. First he turned himself into a tick, and hid himself in Dapplegrim's left nostril; and the Princess went about hunting him everywhere, high and low; at last she wanted to go into Dapplegrim's stall, but he began to bite and kick, so that she daren't go near him, and so she couldn't find the lad.

'Well,' she said, 'since I can't find you, you must show where you are yourself.' And in a trice the lad stood there on the stable floor.

The second time Dapplegrim told him again what to do; and then he turned himself into a clod of earth, and stuck himself between Dapple's hoof and shoe on the near forefoot. So the princess hunted up and down, out and in, everywhere; at last she came into the stable, and wanted to go into Dapplegrim's loose-box. This time he let her come up to him, and she pried high and low, but under his hoofs she couldn't come, for he stood firm as a rock on his feet, and so she couldn't find the lad.

'Well, you must just show yourself, for I'm sure I can't find you,' said the princess, and as she spoke the lad stood by her side on the stable floor.

'Now you are mine indeed,' said the lad. 'For now you can see I'm fated to have you.' This he said both to the father and daughter.

'Yes; it is so fated,' said the king. 'So it must be.' Then they got ready the wedding in right down earnest, and lost no time about it; and the lad got on Dapplegrim, and the princess on Dapplegrim's match, and then you may fancy they were not long on their way to the church.

THE SEVEN FOALS

BY G. W. DASENT

Once on a time, there was a poor couple who lived in a wretched hut, far, far away in the wood. How they lived I can't tell, but I'm sure it was from hand to mouth, and hard work even then; but they had three sons, and the youngest of them was Boots, of course, for he did little else than lie there and poke about in the ashes.

So one day the eldest lad said he would go out to earn his bread, and he soon got leave, and wandered out into the world. There he walked and walked the whole day, and when evening drew in, he came to a king's palace, and there stood the king out on the steps, and asked whither he was bound.

'Oh, I'm going about, looking after a place,' said the lad.

'Will you serve me?' asked the king, 'and watch my seven foals. If you can watch them one whole day, and tell me at night what they eat and what they drink, you shall have the princess to wife, and half my kingdom; but if you can't, I'll cut three red stripes out of your back. Do you hear?'

Yes, that was an easy task, the lad thought; he'd do that fast enough, never fear.

So next morning, as soon as the first peep of dawn came, the king's coachman let out the seven foals. Away they went, and the lad after them. You may fancy how they tore over hill and dale, through bush and bog. When the lad had run so a long time, he began to get weary, and when he had held on a while longer, he had more than enough of his watching, and just there, he came to a cleft in a rock, where an old hag sat and spun with a distaff. As soon as she saw the lad who was running after the foals till the sweat ran down his brow, this old hag bawled out: 'Come hither, come hither, my pretty son, and let me comb your hair.'

Yes, the lad was willing enough; so he sat down in the cleft of the rock with the old hag, and laid his head on her lap, and she combed his hair all day whilst he lay there, and stretched his lazy bones.

So, when evening drew on, the lad wanted to go away. 'I may just as well toddle straight home now,' said he, 'for it's no use my going back to the palace.'

'Stop a bit till it's dark,' said the old hag, 'and then the king's foals will pass by here again, and then you can run home with them, and then no one will know that you have lain here all day long, instead of watching the foals.'

So when they came, she gave the lad a flask of water and a clod of turf. Those he was to show to the king, and say that was what his seven foals ate and drank.

'Have you watched true and well the whole day, now?' asked the king, when the lad came before him in the evening.

'Yes, I should think so,' said the lad.

'Then you can tell me what my seven foals eat and drink,' said the king.

'Yes!' and so the lad pulled out the flask of water and the clod of turf, which the old hag had given him.

'Here you see their meat, and here you see their drink,' said the lad.

But then the king saw plain enough how he had watched, and he got so wroth, he ordered his men to chase him away home on the spot; but first they were to cut three red stripes out of his back, and rub salt into them. So when the lad got home again, you may fancy what a temper he was in. He'd gone out once to get a place, he said, but he'd never do so again.

Next day the second son said he would go out into the world to try his luck. His father and mother said 'No,' and bade him look at his brother's back, but the lad wouldn't give in; he held to his own, and at last he got leave to go and set off. So when he had walked the whole day, he, too, came to the king's palace. There stood the king out on the steps, and asked whither he was bound, and when the lad said he was looking about for a place, the king said he might have a place there, and watch his seven foals. But the king laid down the same punishment, and the same reward, as he had settled for his brother. Well, the lad was willing enough; he took the place at once with the king, for he thought he'd soon watch the foals, and tell the king what they ate and drank. So, in the grey of the morning, the coachman let out the seven foals, and off they went again over hill and dale, and the lad after them. But the same thing happened to him as had befallen his brother. When he had run after the foals a long, long time, till he was both warm and weary, he passed by the cleft in a rock, where an old hag sat and spun with a distaff, and she bawled out to the lad: 'Come hither, come hither, my pretty son, and let me comb your hair.'

That the lad thought a good offer, so he let the foals run on their way, and sat down in the cleft with the old hag. There he sat, and there he lay, taking his ease, and stretching his lazy bones the whole day.

When the foals came back at nightfall, he too got a flask of water and clod of turf from the old hag to show to the king. But when the king asked the lad, 'Can you tell me now, what my seven foals eat and drink?' the lad pulled out the flask and the clod, and said, 'Here you see their meat, and here you see their drink.'

Then the king got wroth again, and ordered them to cut three red stripes out of the lad's back, and rub salt in, and chase him home that very minute. And so when the lad got home, he also told how he had fared, and said he had gone out once to get a place, but he'd never do so any more.

The third day Boots wanted to set out; he had a great mind to try and watch the seven foals, he said. The others laughed at him, and made game of him, saying: 'When we fared so ill, you'll do it better – a fine joke; you look like it – you, who have never done anything but lie there and poke about in the ashes.'

'Yes,' said Boots, 'I don't see why I shouldn't go, for I've got it into my head, and can't get it out again.'

And so, in spite of all the jeers of the others and the prayers of the old people, there was no help for it, and Boots set out.

So after he had walked the whole day, he, too, came at dusk to the king's palace. There stood the King out on the steps, and asked whither he was bound.

'Oh,' said Boots, 'I'm going about seeing if I can hear of a place.'

'Whence do you come then?' said the king, for he wanted to know a little more about a person before he took anyone into his service.

So Boots said whence he came, and how he was brother to those two who had watched the king's seven foals, and ended by asking if he might try to watch them next day.

'Oh, stuff!' said the king, for he got quite cross if he even thought of them, 'if you're brother to those two, you're not worth much, I'll be bound. I've had enough of such scamps.'

'Well,' said Boots, but since I've come so far, I may just as well get leave to try, I too.'

'Oh, very well, with all my heart', said the king, 'if you *will* have your back flayed, you're quite welcome.'

'I'd much rather have the princess,' said Boots.

So next morning, at grey of dawn, the coachman let out the seven foals again, and away they went over hill and dale, through bush and bog, and Boots behind them. And so, when he too had run a long while, he came to the cleft in the rock, where the old hag sat, spinning at her distaff. So she bawled out to Boots: 'Come hither, come hither, my pretty son, and let me comb your hair.'

'Don't you wish you may catch me,' said Boots. 'Don't you wish you may catch me,' as he ran along, leaping and jumping, and holding on to one of the foal's tails. And when he had got well past the cleft in the rock, the youngest foal said: 'Jump up on my back, my lad, for we've a long way before us still.' So Boots jumped up on his back.

So they went on, and on, a long, long way.

'Do you see anything now,' asked the foal.

'No,' said Boots. So they went on a good bit farther.

'Do you see anything now?' asked the foal.

'Oh no,' said the lad.

So when they had gone a great, great way farther – I'm sure I can't tell how far – the foal asked again: 'Do you see anything now?'

'Yes,' said Boots, 'now I see something that looks white – just like a tall, big birch trunk.'

'Yes,' said the foal, 'we're going into that trunk.' So when they got to the trunk, the eldest foal took and pushed it on one side, and then they saw a door where it had stood, and inside the door was a little room, and in the room there was scarce anything but a little fireplace and one or two benches, but behind the door hung a great rusty sword and a little pitcher.

'Can you brandish the sword?' asked the Foals. 'Try.' So Boots tried, but he couldn't. Then they made him take a pull at the pitcher; first once, then twice, and then thrice, and then he could wield it like anything.

'Yes,' said the foals, 'now you may take the sword with you, and with it you must cut off all our seven heads on your wedding day, and then we'll be princes again as we were before. For we are brothers of that princess whom you are to have when you can tell the king what we eat and drink, but an ugly troll has thrown this shape over us. Now mind, when you have hewn off our heads, to take care to lay each head at the tail of the trunk which it belonged to before, and then the spell will have no more power over us.'

Yes, Boots promised all that, and then on they went. And when they had travelled a long long way, the foal asked: 'Do you see anything?'

'No,' said Boots. So they travelled a good bit still.

'And now?' asked the foal.

'No, I see nothing,' said Boots. So they travelled many many miles again, over hill and dale.

'Now then,' said the foal, 'do you see anything now?'

'Yes,' said Boots, 'now I see something like a blue stripe, far far away.'

'Yes,' said the foal, 'that's a river we've got to cross.' Over the river was a long, grand bridge, and when they had got over to the other side, they travelled on a long, long way. At last the Foal asked again if Boots didn't see anything.

Yes, this time he saw something that looked black far far away, just as though it were a church steeple.

'Yes,' said the foal, 'that's where we're going to turn in.'

So when the foals got into the churchyard, they became men again, and looked like princes, with such fine clothes that it glistened from them, and so they went into the church, and took the bread and wine from the priest who stood at the altar. And Boots he went in too. And when the priest had laid his hands on the Princes, and given them the blessing, they went out of the church again, and Boots went out too, but he took with him a flask of wine and a wafer. And soon as ever the seven princes came out into the churchyard, they were turned into foals again, and so Boots got up on the back of the youngest, and so they all went back the same way that they had come, only they went much, much faster. First they crossed the bridge, next they passed the trunk, and then they passed the old hag, who sat at the cleft and span, and they went by her so fast, that Boots couldn't hear what the old hag screeched after him, but he heard so much as to know she was in an awful rage.

It was almost dark when they got back to the palace, and the king himself stood out on the steps and waited for them. 'Have you watched well and true the whole day?' said he to Boots.

'I've done my best,' answered Boots.

'Then you can tell me what my seven foals eat and drink,' said the king.

Then Boots pulled out the flask of wine and the wafer, and showed them to the king.

'Here you see their meat, and here you see their drink,' said he.

'Yes,' said the king. 'You have watched true and well, and you shall have the princess and half the kingdom.'

So they made ready the wedding feast, and the king said it should be such a grand one, it should be the talk far and near.

But when they sat down to the bridal feast, the bridegroom got up and went down to the stable, for he said he had forgotten something, and must go to fetch it. And when he got down there, he did as the foals had said, and hewed their heads off, all seven, the eldest first, and the others after him, and at the same time he took care to lay each head at the tail of the foal to which it belonged. And as he did this, lo, they all became princes again.

So when he went into the bridal hall with the seven princes, the king was so glad he both kissed Boots and patted him on the back, and his bride was still more glad of him than she had been before.

'Half the kingdom you have got already,' said the king, 'and the other half you shall have after my death; for my sons can easily get themselves lands and wealth, now they are princes again.'

And so, like enough, there was mirth and fun at that wedding. I was there too, but there was no one to care for poor me, and so I got nothing but a bit of bread and butter, and I laid it down on the stove, and the bread was burnt and the butter ran, and so I didn't get even the smallest crumb. Wasn't that a great shame?

HOW A LAD STOLE THE GIANT'S TREASURE

BY CHARLES JOHN TIBBITS

Once upon a time, there lived a peasant who had three sons. The two elder ones used to go with him to the field and to the forest, and helped him in his work, but the youngest remained at home with his mother, to help her in the house. His brothers despised him for doing this, and whenever they had a chance they used him badly.

At length the father and mother died, and the sons divided the property among them. As might have been looked for, the elder brothers took all that was of any value for themselves, leaving nothing to the youngest but an old cracked kneading-trough, which neither of them thought worth the having.

'The old trough,' said one of the brothers, 'will do very well for our young brother, for he is always baking and scrubbing.'

The boy thought this, as was only natural, a poor thing to inherit, but he could do nothing, and he now recognised that it would be no use his remaining at home, so he wished his brothers goodbye, and went off to seek his fortune. On coming to the side of a lake he made his trough watertight with oakum, and converted it into a little boat. Then he found two sticks, and using these as oars, rowed away.

When he had crossed the water, he saw a large palace, and entering it, he asked to speak with the king. The king questioned him respecting his family and the purpose of his visit.

'I,' said the boy, 'am the son of a poor peasant, and all I have in the world is an old kneading-trough. I have come here to seek work.'

The king laughed when he heard this.

'Indeed,' said he, 'you have not inherited much, but fortune works many a change.'

He took the lad to be one of his servants, and he became a favourite for his courage and honesty.

Now the king who owned this palace had an only daughter, who was so beautiful and so clever that she was talked of all through the kingdom, and many came from the east and from the west to ask her hand in marriage. The princess, however, rejected them all, saying that none should have her for his wife unless he brought her for a wedding present four valuable things belonging to a giant who lived on the other side of the lake. These four treasures were a gold sword, three gold hens, a gold lantern and a gold harp.

Many kings' sons and many good warriors tried to win these treasures, but none of them came back, for the giant caught them all and eat them. The king was very sorrowful, for he feared that at this rate his daughter would never get a husband, and so he would not have a son-in-law to whom he could leave his kingdom.

The boy, when he heard of this, thought that it might be well worth his while to try to win the king's beautiful daughter. So he went to the king one day, and told him what he meant to do. When the king heard him, he got angry and said, 'Do you think that you, who are only a servant, can do what great warriors have failed in?'

The boy, however, was not to be dissuaded, and begged him so to let him go that at last the king grew calmer and gave him his permission. 'But,' said he, 'you will lose your life, and I shall be sorry to miss you.' With that they parted.

The boy went down to the shore of the lake, and, having found his trough, he looked it over very closely. Then he got into it and rowed across the lake, and, coming to the giant's dwelling, he hid himself and stayed the night there.

Very early in the morning, before it was light, the giant went to his barn and began to thrash, making such a noise that the mountains all around echoed again. When the boy heard this he collected some stones and put them in his pouch. Then he climbed up on to the roof of the barn and made a little hole so that he could look in. Now the giant had by his side his golden sword, which had the strange property that it clanked whenever the giant was angry. While the giant was busy thrashing at full speed, the boy threw a little stone which hit the sword, and caused it to clank.

'Why do you clank?' asked the giant. 'I am not angry.'

He went on thrashing, but the next moment the sword clanked again. Once more the giant pursued his work, and the sword clanked a third time. Then the giant got so angry that he undid the belt, and threw the sword out of the barn door.

'Lie there,' said he, 'till I have done my thrashing.'

The lad waited no longer, but slipping down from the roof seized on the sword, ran to his boat, and rowed across the water. On reaching the other side he hid his treasure, and was full of glee at the success of his adventure.

The next day he filled his pouch with corn, put a bundle of bast-twine in his boat, and once more set off to the giant's dwelling. He lay hiding for a time, and then he saw the giant's three golden hens walking about on the shore, and spreading their feathers, which sparkled beautifully in the bright sunshine. He was soon near them, and began to softly lead them on, scattering corn for them out of his pouch. While they were picking the boy gradually led them to the water, till at last he got them into his little boat. Then he jumped in himself, secured the fowl with his twine, pushed out from the shore, and rowed as quickly as he could to the other side of the water.

The third day he put some lumps of salt into his pouch, and again rowed across the lake. As night came on he noticed how the smoke rose from the giant's dwelling, and concluded that the giant's wife was busy getting ready his food. He crept up on to the roof, and, looking down through the hole by which the smoke escaped, saw a large caldron boiling on the fire. Then he took the lumps of salt out of his pouch, and threw them one by one into the pot. Having done this, he crept down from the roof, and waited to see what would follow.

Soon after the giant's wife took the caldron off the fire, poured out the porridge into a bowl, and put it on the table. The giant was hungry, and he fell to at once, but scarcely had he tasted the porridge when he found it too salt. He got very angry, and started from his seat. The old woman made what excuse she could, and said that the porridge must be good, but the giant declared he would eat no more of the stuff, and told her to taste it for herself. She did so, and pulled a terrible face, for she had never in her life tasted such abominable stuff.

There was nothing for it but she must make some new porridge. So she seized a can, took the gold lantern down from the wall, and went as fast as she could to the well to draw some water. She put the lantern down by the side of the well, and was stooping down to get the water, when the boy ran to her, and, laying hold of her by the feet, threw her head over heels into the well. He seized hold of the golden lantern, ran away as fast as he could to his boat, and rowed across the water in safety.

The giant sat for a long time wondering why his wife was away so long. At last he went to look for her, but nothing could he see of her. Then he heard a splashing in the well, and finding she was in the water, he, with a lot of work, got her out.

'Where is my gold lantern?' was the first thing he asked, as the old woman came round a little.

'I don't know,' answered she. 'Somebody came, caught me by the feet, and threw me into the well.'

The giant was very angry at this.

'Three of my treasures,' said he, 'have gone, and I have now only my golden harp left. But, whoever the thief may be, he shall not have that; I will keep that safe under twelve locks.'

While these things occurred at the giant's dwelling, the boy sat on the other side of the water, rejoicing that he had got on so well.

The most difficult task, however, had yet to be done, and for a long time he thought over how he could get the golden harp. At length he determined to row over to the giant's place and see if fortune would favour him.

No sooner said than done. He rowed over and went to a hiding place. The giant had, however, been on the watch, and had seen him. So he rushed forward in a terrible rage and seized the boy, saying, 'So I have caught you at last, you young rascal. You it was who stole my sword, my three gold hens and my gold lantern.'

The boy was terribly afraid, for he thought his last hour was come.

'Spare my life, father,' said he humbly, 'and I will never come here again.'

'No,' replied the giant, 'I will do the same with you as with the others. No one slips alive out of my hands.'

He then shut the boy up in a sty, and fed him with nuts and sweet milk, so as to get him nice and fat preparatory to killing and eating him.

The lad was a prisoner, but he ate and drank and made himself as easy as he could. After some time the giant wanted to find out if he were fat enough to be killed. So he went to the sty, made a little hole in the wall, and told the boy to put his finger through it. The lad knew what he wanted; so instead of putting out his finger he poked out a little peeled alder twig. The giant cut the twig, and the red sap ran out. Then he thought the boy must be yet very lean since his flesh was so hard, so he caused a greater supply of milk and nuts to be given to him.

Some time after, the giant again visited the sty, and ordered the boy to put his finger through the hole in the wall. The lad now poked out a cabbage-stalk, and the giant, having cut it with his knife, concluded that the lad must be fat enough, his flesh seemed so soft.

The next morning the giant said to his wife, 'The boy seems to be fat enough now, mother. Take him then today, and bake him in the oven, while I go and ask our kinsfolk to the feast.'

The old woman promised to do what her husband told her. So, having heated the oven, she dragged out the boy to bake him.

'Sit on the shovel,' said she.

The boy did so, but when the old woman raised the shovel the boy always fell off. So they went on many times. At last the giantess got angry, and scolded the boy for being so awkward;

the lad excused himself, saying that he did not know the way to sit on the shovel.

'Look at me,' said the woman, 'I will show you.'

So she sat herself down on the shovel, bending her back and drawing up her knees. No sooner was she seated than the boy, seizing hold of the handle, pushed her into the oven and slammed the door to. Then he took the woman's fur cloak, stuffed it out with straw, and laid it on the bed. Seizing the giant's bunch of keys, he opened the twelve locks, snatched up the golden harp, and ran down to his boat, which he had hidden among the flags on the shore.

The giant soon afterwards came home.

'Where can my wife be?' said he. 'No doubt she has lain down to sleep a bit. Ah! I thought so.'

The old woman, however, slept a long while, and the giant could not wake her, though he was now expecting his friends to arrive.

'Wake up, mother,' cried he, but no one replied. He called again, but there was no response. He got angry, and, going to the bed, he gave the fur cloak a good shake. Then he found that it was not his wife, but only a bundle of straw put in her clothes. At this the giant grew alarmed, and he ran off to look after his golden harp. He found his keys gone, the twelve locks undone, and the harp missing. He went to the oven and opened the door to see how the meat for the feast was going on. Behold! There sat his wife, baked, and grinning at him.

Then the giant was almost mad with grief and rage, and he rushed out to seek the lad who had done him all this mischief. He came down to the edge of the water and found him sitting in his boat, playing on the harp. The music came over the water, and the gold strings shone wonderfully in the sunshine. The giant jumped into the water after the boy, but finding that it was too deep, he laid himself down, and began to drink the water in order to make the lake shallower. He drank with all his might, and by this means set up a current which drew the boat nearer and nearer to the shore. Just when he was going to lay hold of it he burst, for he had drunk too much – and there was an end of him.

The giant lay dead on the shore, and the boy moved away across the lake, full of joy and happiness. When he came to land, he combed his golden hair, put on fine clothes, fastened the giant's gold sword by his side, and, taking the gold harp in one hand and the gold lantern in the other, he led the gold fowl after him, and went to the king, who was sitting in the great hall of the palace surrounded by his courtiers. When the king saw the boy he was heartily glad. The lad went to the king's beautiful daughter, saluted her courteously, and laid the giant's treasures before her. Then there was great joy in the palace, that the princess had after all got the giant's treasures and so bold and handsome a bridegroom. The wedding was celebrated soon after with very much splendour and rejoicing; and when the king died the lad succeeded him, ruling over all the land both long and happily.

I know no more respecting them.

THE MAGICIAN'S DAUGHTER

BY CHARLES JOHN TIBBITS

Just on the Finland frontiers there is situated a high mountain, which, on the Swedish side, is covered with beautiful copsewood, and on the other with dark pine trees, so closely ranked together, and so luxuriant in shade, that one might almost say the smallest bird could not find its way through the thickets. Below the copsewood there stands a chapel with the image of St. George, as guardian of the land and as a defence against dragons, if there be such, and other monsters of paganism, while, on the other side, on the borders of the dark firwood, are certain cottages inhabited by wicked sorcerers, who have, moreover, a cave cut so deep into the mountain that it joins with the bottomless abyss, whence come all the demons that assist them. The Swedish Christians who dwelt in the neighbourhood of this mountain thought it would be necessary, besides the chapel and statue of St. George, to choose some living protector, and therefore selected an ancient warrior, highly renowned for his prowess in the battlefield, who had, in his old age, become a monk. When this man went to take up his abode upon the mountains, his only son (for he had formerly lived as a married man in the world) would on no account leave him, but lived there also, assisting his father in his duties as watcher, and in the exercises of prayer and penitence, fully equalling the example that was now afforded him as he had formerly done his example as a soldier.

The life led by those two valiant champions is said to have been most admirable and pious.

Once on a time, it happened that the young hero went out to cut wood in the forest. He bore a sharp axe on his shoulders, and was, besides, girded with a great sword; for as the woods were not only full of wild beasts, but also haunted by wicked men, the pious hermits took the precaution of always going armed. While the good youth was forcing his way through the thickest of the copsewood, and already beheld over it the pointed tops of the fir trees (for he was close on the Finnish frontier), there rushed out against him a great white wolf, so that he had only just time enough to leap to one side, and not being able immediately to draw his sword, he flung his axe at his assailant. The blow was so well aimed that it struck one of the wolf's forelegs, and the animal, being sorely wounded, limped back, with a yell of anguish, into the wood. The young hermit warrior, however, thought to himself, 'It is not enough that I am rescued, but I must take such measures that no one else may in future be injured, or even terrified by this wild beast.'

So he rushed in as fast as possible among the fir trees, and inflicted such a vehement blow with his sword on the wolf's head, that the animal, groaning piteously, fell to the ground. Hereupon there came over the young man all at once a strange mood of regret and compassion for his poor victim. Instead of putting it immediately to death, he bound up the wounds as well as he could with moss and twigs of trees, placed it on a sort of canvas sling on which he was in the habit of carrying great fagots, and with much labour brought it home, in hopes that he might be able at last to cure and tame his fallen adversary. He did not find his father in the cottage, and it was not without some fear and anxiety that he laid the wolf on his own bed, which was made of moss and rushes, and over which he had nailed St. George and the Dragon. He then turned to the fireplace of the small hut, in order to prepare a healing salve for the wounds. While he was thus occupied, how much was he astonished to hear the moanings and lamentations of a human voice from the bed on which he had just before deposited the wolf. On returning thither his wonder was inexpressible on perceiving, instead of the frightful wild beast, a most beautiful damsel, on whose head the wound which he had inflicted was bleeding through her fine golden hair, and whose right arm, in all its grace and snow-white luxuriance, was stretched out motionless, for it had been broken by the blow from his axe.

'Pray,' said she, 'have pity, and do not kill me outright. The little life that I have still left is, indeed, painful enough, and may not last long; yet, sad as my condition is, it is yet tenfold better than death.'

The young man then sat down weeping beside her, and she explained to him that she was the daughter of a magician, on the other side of the mountain, who had sent her out in the shape of a wolf to collect plants from places which, in her own proper form, she could not have reached. It was but in terror she had made that violent spring which the youth had mistaken for an attack on him, when her only wish had been to pass by him.

'But you directly broke my right arm,' said she, 'though I had no evil design against you.'

How she had now regained her proper shape she could not imagine, but to the youth it was quite clear that the picture of St. George and the Dragon had broken the spell by which the poor girl had been transformed.

While the son was thus occupied, the old man returned home, and soon heard all that had occurred, perceiving, at the same time, that if the young pagan wanderer had been released from the spells by which she had been bound, the youth was, in his turn, enchanted and spellbound by her beauty and amiable behaviour.

From that moment he exerted himself to the utmost for the welfare of her soul, endeavouring to convert her to Christianity, while his son attended to the cure of her wounds; and, as their endeavours were on both sides successful, it was resolved that the lovers should be united in marriage, for the youth had not restricted himself by any monastic vows.

The magician's daughter was now restored to perfect health, and a day had been appointed for her baptism and marriage.

It happened that one evening the bride and bridegroom went to take a pleasure walk through the woods. The sun was yet high in the west, and shone so fervently through the beech trees on the green turf that they could never resolve on turning home, but went still deeper and deeper into the forest. Then the bride told him stories of her early life, and sang old songs which she had learned when a child, and which sounded beautifully amid the woodland solitude. Though the words were such that they could not be agreeable to the youth's ears (for she had learned them among her pagan and wicked relations), yet he could not interrupt her, first, because he loved her so dearly, and, secondly, because she sang in a voice so clear and sweet that the whole forest seemed to rejoice in her music. At last, however, the pointed heads of the pine trees again became visible, and the youth wished to turn back, in order that he might not come again too near the hated Finnish frontier. His bride, however, said to him, 'Dearest Conrad, why should we not walk on a little further? I would gladly see the very place where you so cruelly wounded me on the head and arm, and made me prisoner, all which has, in the end contributed to my happiness. Methinks we are now very near the spot.'

Accordingly they sought about here and there until at last the twilight fell dim and heavy on the dense woods. The sun had long since set. The moon, however, had risen, and, as a light broke forth, the lovers stood on the Finnish frontier, or rather they must have gone already some distance beyond it, for the bridegroom was exceedingly terrified when he found his cap lifted from his head, as if by human hand, though he saw only the branch of a fir tree. Immediately thereafter the whole air around them was filled with strange and supernatural beings – witches, devils, dwarfs, horned-owls, fire-eyed cats, and a thousand other wretches that could not be named and described, whirled around them as if dancing to rapid music. When the bride had looked on for a while, she broke out into loud laughter, and at last began to dance furiously along with them. The poor bridegroom might shout and pray as much and as earnestly as he would, for she never attended to him, but at last transformed herself in a manner so extraordinary that he could not distinguish her from the other dancers. He thought, however, that he had kept his eyes upon her, and seized on one of the dancers; but alas, it was only a horrible spectre which held him fast, and threw its wide waving shroud around him, so that he could not make his escape, while, at the same time, some of the subterraneous black demons pulled at his legs, and wanted to bear him down along with them into their bottomless caves.

Fortunately he happened at that moment to cross himself and call on the name of the Saviour, upon which the whole of this vile assembly fell into confusion. They howled aloud and ran off in all directions, while Conrad in the meantime saved himself by recrossing the frontier, and getting under the protection of the Swedish copsewood. His beautiful bride, however, was completely lost; and by no endeavours could he ever obtain her again, though he often came to the Finnish border, called out her name aloud, wept and prayed, but all in vain. Many times, it is true, he saw her floating about through the pine trees, as if in chase, but she was always accompanied by a train of frightful creatures, and she herself also looked wild and disfigured. For the most part she never noticed Conrad, but if she could not help fixing her eyes upon him, she laughed so immoderately, and in a mood of merriment so strange and unnatural, that he was terrified and made the sign of the cross, whereupon she always fled away, howling, into one of the thickets.

Conrad fell more and more into melancholy abstraction, hardly ever spoke, and though he had given over his vain walks into the forest, yet if one asked him a question, the only answer he returned was, 'Ay, she is gone away beyond the mountains,' so little did he know or remember of any other object in the world but the lost beauty.

At last he died of grief; and according to a request which he had once made, his father prepared a grave for him on the place where the bride was found and lost, though during the fulfilment of this duty he had enough to do – one while in contending with his crucifix against evil spirits, and at another, with his sword against wild beasts, which were no doubt sent thither by the magicians to attack and annoy him. At length, however, he brought his task to an end, and thereafter it seemed as if the bride mourned for the youth's untimely death, for there was heard often a sound of howling and lamentation at the grave. For the most part, indeed, this voice is like the voices of wolves, yet, at the same time, human accents are to be distinguished, and I myself have often listened thereto on dark winter nights.

Alas, that the poor maiden should have ventured again so near the accursed paths she had once renounced! A few steps in the backward course, and all is lost!

THE MEAL OF FROTHI

BY CHARLES JOHN TIBBITS

Gold is called by the poets the meal of Frothi, and the origin of the term is found in this story.

Odin had a son named Skioldr who settled and reigned in the land which is now called Denmark, but was then called Gotland. Skioldr had a son named Frithleif, who reigned after him. Frithleif's son was called Frothi, and succeeded him on the throne. At the time that the Emperor Augustus made peace over the whole world, Christ was born, but as Frothi was the most powerful of all the monarchs of the north, that peace, wherever the Danish language was spoken, was imputed to him, and the Northmen called it Frothi's peace.

At that time no man hurt another, even if he found the murderer of his father or brother, loose or bound. Theft and robbery were then unknown, insomuch that a gold armlet lay for a long time untouched in Jalangursheath.

Frothi chanced to go on a friendly visit to a certain king in Sweden, named Fiolnir, and there purchased two female slaves, called Fenia and Menia, equally distinguished for their stature and strength. In those days there were found in Denmark two quern-stones of such a size, that no one was able to move them, and these millstones were endued with such virtue, that the quern in grinding produced whatever the grinder wished for. The quern was called Grotti. He who presented this quern to Frothi was called Hengikioptr (hanging-chops). King Frothi caused these slaves to be brought to the quern, and ordered them to grind gold, peace and prosperity for Frothi. The king allowed them no longer rest or sleep than while the cuckoo was silent or a verse could be recited. Then they are said to have sung the lay called Grotta-Savngr, and before they ended their song to have ground a hostile army against Frothi, insomuch, that a certain sea-king, called Mysingr, arriving the same night, slew Frothi, taking great spoil. And so ended Frothi's peace.

Mysingr took with him the quern, Grotti, with Fenia and Menia, and ordered them to grind salt. About midnight they asked Mysingr whether he had salt enough. On his ordering them to go on grinding, they went on a little longer till the ship sank under the weight of the salt. A whirlpool was produced, where the waves are sucked up by the mill-eye, and the waters of the sea have been salty ever since.

HOLGER DANSKE

BY CHARLES JOHN TIBBITS

The Danish peasantry of the present day relate many wonderful things of an ancient hero whom they name Holger Danske, i.e. Danish Holger, and to whom they ascribe wonderful strength and dimensions.

Holger Danske came one time to a town named Bagsvoer, in the isle of Zealand, where, being in want of a new suit of clothes, he sent for twelve tailors to make them. He was so tall that they were obliged to set ladders to his back and shoulders to take his measure. They measured and measured away, but unluckily a man, who was on the top of one of the ladders, happened, as he was cutting a mark in the measure, to give Holger's ear a clip with the scissors. Holger, forgetting what was going on, thinking that he was being bitten by a flea, put up his hand and crushed the unlucky tailor to death between his fingers.

It is also said that a witch one time gave him a pair of spectacles which would enable him to see through the ground. He lay down at a place not far from Copenhagen to make a trial of their powers, and as he put his face close to the ground, he left in it the mark of his spectacles, which mark is to be seen at this very day, and the size of it proves what a goodly pair they must have been.

Tradition does not say at what time it was that this mighty hero honoured the isles of the Baltic with his actual presence, but, in return, it informs us that Holger, like so many other heroes of renown, 'is not dead, but sleepeth'. The clang of arms, we are told, was frequently heard under the castle of Cronberg, but in all Denmark no one could be found hardy enough to penetrate the subterranean recesses and ascertain the cause. At length a slave, who had been condemned to death, was offered his life and a pardon if he would go down, proceed through the subterranean passage as far as it went, and bring an account of what he should meet there. He accordingly descended, and went along till he came to a great iron door, which opened of itself the instant he knocked at it, and he beheld before him a deep vault. From the roof in the centre hung a lamp whose flame was nearly extinct, and beneath was a huge great stone table, around which sat steel-clad warriors, bowed down over it, each with his head on his crossed arms. He who was seated at the head of the board then raised himself up. This was Holger Danske. When he had lifted his head up from off his arms, the stone table split throughout, for his beard was grown into it.

'Give me thy hand,' said he to the intruder.

The slave feared to trust his hand in the grasp of the ancient warrior, and he reached him the end of an iron bar which he had brought with him. Holger squeezed it so hard, that the mark of his hand remained in it. He let it go at last, saying, 'Well! I am glad to find there are still men in Denmark.'

ORIGIN OF TIIS LAKE

BY CHARLES JOHN TIBBITS

A troll had once taken up his abode near the village of Kund, in the high bank on which the church now stands, but when the people about there had become pious, and went constantly to church, the troll was dreadfully annoyed by their almost incessant ringing of bells in the steeple of the church. He was at last obliged, in consequence of it, to take his departure, for nothing has more contributed to the emigration of the troll-folk out of the country, than the increasing piety of the people, and their taking to bell-ringing. The troll of Kund accordingly quitted the country, and went over to Funen, where he lived for some time in peace and quiet. Now it chanced that a man who had lately settled in the town of Kund, coming to Funen on business, met this same troll on the road.

'Where do you live?' asked the troll.

Now there was nothing whatever about the troll unlike a man, so he answered him, as was the truth, 'I am from the town of Kund.'

'So?' said the troll, 'I don't know you then. And yet I think I know every man in Kund. Will you, however,' said he, 'be so kind as to take a letter for me back with you to Kund?'

The man, of course, said he had no objection.

The troll put a letter into his pocket and charged him strictly not to take it out until he came to Kund church. Then he was to throw it over the churchyard wall, and the person for whom it was intended would get it.

The troll then went away in great haste, and with him the letter went entirely out of the man's mind. But when he was come back to Zealand he sat down by the meadow where Tiis lake now is, and suddenly recollected the troll's letter. He felt a great desire to look at it at least, so he took it out of his pocket and sat a while with it in his hands, when suddenly there began to dribble a little water out of the seal. The letter now unfolded itself and the water came out faster and faster, and it was with the utmost difficulty the poor man was able to save his life, for the malicious troll had enclosed a whole lake in the letter.

The troll, it is plain, had thought to avenge himself on Kund church by destroying it in this manner, but God ordered it so that the lake chanced to run out in the great meadow where it now stands.

TALES OF THE NISSES

BY CHARLES JOHN TIBBITS

The Nis is the same being that is called Kobold in Germany, and Brownie in Scotland. He is in Denmark and Norway also called Nisse god dreng (Nissè good lad), and in Sweden, Tomtegubbe (the old man of the house).

He is of the dwarf family, and resembles them in appearance, and, like them, has the command of money, and the same dislike of noise and tumult.

His usual dress is grey, with a pointed red cap, but on Michaelmas Day he wears a round hat like those of the peasants.

No farmhouse goes on well without there is a Nis in it, and well is it for the maids and the men when they are in favour with him. They may go to their beds and give themselves no trouble about their work, and yet in the morning the maids will find the kitchen swept up, and water brought in; and the men will find the horses in the stable well cleaned and curried, and perhaps a supply of corn cribbed for them from the neighbours' barns.

There was a Nis in a house in Jutland. He every evening got his groute at the regular time, and he, in return, used to help both the men and the maids, and looked to the interest of the master of the house in every respect.

There came one time a mischievous boy to live at service in this house, and his great delight was, whenever he got an opportunity, to give the Nis all the annoyance in his power.

Late one evening, when everything was quiet in the house, the Nis took his little wooden dish, and was just going to eat his supper, when he perceived that the boy had put the butter at the bottom and had concealed it, in hopes that he might eat the groute first, and then find the butter when all the groute was gone. He accordingly set about thinking how he might repay the boy in kind. After pondering a little he went up into the loft where a man and the boy were lying asleep in the same bed. The Nis whisked off the bedclothes, and when he saw the little boy by the tall man, he said, 'Short and long don't match,' and with this word he took the boy by the legs and dragged him down to the man's feet. He then went up to the head of the bed, and: 'Short and long don't match,' said he again, and then he dragged the boy up to the man's head. Do what he would he could not succeed in making the boy as long as the man, but persisted in dragging him up and down in the bed, and continued at this work the whole night long till it was broad daylight.

By this time he was well tired, so he crept up on the window stool, and sat with his legs dangling down into the yard. The house dog – for all dogs have a great enmity to the Nis – as soon as he saw him began to bark at him, which afforded him much amusement, as the dog could not get up to him. So he put down first one leg and then the other, and teased the dog, saying, 'Look at my little leg. Look at my little leg!'

In the meantime the boy had awoke, and had stolen up behind him, and, while the Nis was least thinking of it, and was going on with his 'Look at my little leg', the boy tumbled him down into the yard to the dog, crying out at the same time, 'Look at the whole of him now!'

* * *

There lived a man in Thyrsting, in Jutland, who had a Nis in his barn. This Nis used to attend to his cattle, and at night he would steal fodder for them from the neighbours, so that this farmer had the best fed and most thriving cattle in the country.

One time the boy went along with the Nis to Fugleriis to steal corn. The Nis took as much as he thought he could well carry, but the boy was more covetous, and said, 'Oh! take more. Sure, we can rest now and then!'

'Rest!' said the Nis. 'Rest! And what is rest?'

'Do what I tell you,' replied the boy. 'Take more, and we shall find rest when we get out of this.'

The Nis took more, and they went away with it, but when they came to the lands of Thyrsting, the Nis grew tired, and then the boy said to him, 'Here now is rest!' and they both sat down on the side of a little hill.

'If I had known,' said the Nis, as they sat. 'If I had known that rest was so good, I'd have carried off all that was in the barn.'

It happened, some time after, that the boy and the Nis were no longer friends, and as the Nis was sitting one day in the granary-window with his legs hanging out into the yard, the boy ran at him and tumbled him back into the granary. The Nis was revenged on him that very night, for when the boy was gone to bed he stole down to where he was lying and carried him as he was into the yard. Then he laid two pieces of wood across the well and put him lying on them, expecting that when he awoke he would fall, from the fright, into the well and be drowned. He was, however, disappointed, for the boy came off without injury.

* * *

There was a man who lived in the town of Tirup who had a very handsome white mare. This mare had for many years belonged to the same family, and there was a Nis attached to her who brought luck to the place.

This Nis was so fond of the mare that he could hardly endure to let them put her to any kind of work, and he used to come himself every night and feed her of the best; and for this purpose he usually brought a superfluity of corn, both thrashed and in the straw, from the neighbours' barns. All the rest of the cattle enjoyed the advantage, and they were all kept in exceedingly good condition.

It happened at last that the farmhouse passed into the hands of a new owner, who refused to put any faith in what they told him about the mare, so the luck speedily left the place, and went after the mare to a poor neighbour who had bought her. Within five days after his purchase, the poor farmer began to find his circumstances gradually improving, while the income of the other, day after day, fell away and diminished at such a rate that he was hard set to make both ends meet.

If now the man who had got the mare had only known how to be quiet and enjoy the good times that were come upon him, he and his children and his children's children after him would have been in flourishing circumstances till this very day. But when he saw the quantity of corn that came every night to his barn, he could not resist his desire to get a sight of the Nis. So he concealed himself one evening at nightfall in the stable, and as soon as it was midnight he saw how the Nis came from his neighbour's barn and brought a sackful of corn with him. It was now unavoidable that the Nis should get a sight of the man who was watching, so he, with evident marks of grief, gave the mare her food for the last time, cleaned and dressed her to the best of his ability, and when he had done, turned round to where the man was lying, and bid him farewell.

From that day forward the circumstances of both the neighbours were on an equality, for each now kept his own.

THE DWARFS' BANQUET

BY CHARLES JOHN TIBBITS

There lived in Norway, not far from the city of Trondheim, a powerful man who was blessed with all the goods of fortune. A part of the surrounding country was his property, numerous herds fed on his pastures, and a great retinue and a crowd of servants adorned his mansion. He had an only daughter, called Aslog, the fame of whose beauty spread far and wide. The greatest men of the country sought her, but all were alike unsuccessful in their suit, and he who had come full of confidence and joy, rode away home silent and melancholy. Her father, who thought his daughter delayed her choice only to select, forbore to interfere, and exulted in her prudence, but when at length the richest and noblest tried their fortune with as little success as the rest, he grew angry and called his daughter, and said to her, 'Hitherto I have left you to your free choice, but since I see that you reject all without any distinction, and the very best of your suitors seems not good enough for you, I will keep measures no longer with you. What! Shall my family become extinct, and my inheritance pass away into the hands of strangers? I will break your stubborn spirit. I give you now till the festival of the great winternight. Make your choice by that time, or prepare to accept him whom I shall fix on.'

Aslog loved a youth named Orm, handsome as he was brave and noble. She loved him with her whole soul, and she would sooner die than bestow her hand on another. But Orm was poor, and poverty compelled him to serve in the mansion of her father. Aslog's partiality for him was kept a secret, for her father's pride of power and wealth was such that he would never have given his consent to a union with so humble a man.

When Aslog saw the darkness of his countenance, and heard his angry words, she turned pale as death, for she knew his temper, and doubted not that he would put his threats into execution. Without uttering a word in reply, she retired to her chamber, and thought deeply but in vain how to avert the dark storm that hung over her. The great festival approached nearer and nearer, and her anguish increased every day.

At last the lovers resolved on flight.

'I know,' said Orm, 'a secure place where we may remain undiscovered until we find an opportunity of quitting the country.'

At night, when all were asleep, Orm led the trembling Aslog over the snow and ice-fields away to the mountains. The moon and the stars, sparkling still brighter in the cold winter's night, lighted them on their way. They had under their arms a few articles of dress and some skins of animals, which were all they could carry. They ascended the mountains the whole night long till they reached a lonely spot enclosed with lofty rocks. Here Orm conducted the weary Aslog into a cave, the low and narrow entrance to which was hardly perceptible, but it soon enlarged to a great hall, reaching deep into the mountain. He kindled a fire, and they now, reposing on their skins, sat in the deepest solitude far away from all the world.

Orm was the first who had discovered this cave, which is shown to this very day, and as no one knew anything of it, they were safe from the pursuit of Aslog's father. They passed the whole winter in this retirement. Orm used to go a-hunting, and

Aslog stayed at home in the cave, minded the fire, and prepared the necessary food. Frequently did she mount the points of the rocks, but her eyes wandered as far as they could reach only over glittering snow-fields.

The spring now came on: the woods were green, the meadows put on their various colours, and Aslog could but rarely, and with circumspection, venture to leave the cave. One evening Orm came in with the intelligence that he had recognised her father's servants in the distance, and that he could hardly have been unobserved by them whose eyes were as good as his own.

'They will surround this place,' continued he, 'and never rest till they have found us. We must quit our retreat then without a minute's delay.'

They accordingly descended on the other side of the mountain, and reached the strand, where they fortunately found a boat. Orm shoved off, and the boat drove into the open sea. They had escaped their pursuers, but they were now exposed to dangers of another kind. Whither should they turn themselves? They could not venture to land, for Aslog's father was lord of the whole coast, and they would infallibly fall into his hands. Nothing then remained for them but to commit their bark to the wind and waves. They drove along the entire night. At break of day the coast had disappeared, and they saw nothing but the sky above, the sea beneath, and the waves that rose and fell. They had not brought one morsel of food with them, and thirst and hunger began now to torment them. Three days did they toss about in this state of misery, and Aslog, faint and exhausted, saw nothing but certain death before her.

At length, on the evening of the third day, they discovered an island of tolerable magnitude, and surrounded by a number of smaller ones. Orm immediately steered for it, but just as he came near to it there suddenly arose a violent wind, and the sea rolled higher and higher against him. He turned about with a view of approaching it on another side, but with no better success. His vessel, as often as he approached the island, was driven back as if by an invisible power.

'Lord God!' cried he, and blessed himself and looked on poor Aslog, who seemed to be dying of weakness before his eyes.

Scarcely had the exclamation passed his lips when the storm ceased, the waves subsided, and the vessel came to the shore without encountering any hindrance. Orm jumped out on the beach. Some mussels that he found upon the strand strengthened and revived the exhausted Aslog so that she was soon able to leave the boat.

The island was overgrown with low dwarf shrubs, and seemed to be uninhabited; but when they had got about the middle of it, they discovered a house reaching but a little above the ground, and appearing to be half under the surface of the earth. In the hope of meeting human beings and assistance, the wanderers approached it. They listened if they could hear any noise, but the most perfect silence reigned there. Orm at length opened the door, and with his companion walked in; but what was their surprise to find everything regulated and arranged as if for inhabitants, yet not a single living creature visible. The fire was burning on the hearth in the middle of the room, and a kettle with fish hung on it, apparently only waiting for someone to take it off and eat. The beds were made and ready to receive their weary tenants. Orm and Aslog stood for some time dubious, and looked on with a certain degree of awe, but at last, overcome with hunger, they took up the food and ate. When they had satisfied their appetites, and still in the last beams of the setting sun, which now streamed over the island far and wide, discovered no human being, they gave way to weariness, and laid themselves in the beds to which they had been so long strangers.

They had expected to be awakened in the night by the owners of the house on their return home, but their expectation was not fulfilled. They slept undisturbed till the morning sun shone in upon them. No one appeared on any of the following days, and it seemed as if some invisible power had made ready the house for their reception. They spent the whole summer in perfect happiness. They were, to be sure, solitary, yet they did not miss mankind. The wild birds' eggs and the fish they caught yielded them provisions in abundance.

When autumn came, Aslog presented Orm with a son. In the midst of their joy at his appearance they were surprised by a wonderful apparition. The door opened on a sudden, and an old woman stepped in. She had on her a handsome blue dress. There was something proud, but at the same time strange and surprising in her appearance.

'Do not be afraid at my unexpected appearance,' said she. I am the owner of this house, and I thank you for the clean and neat state in which you have kept it, and for the good order in which I find everything with you. I would willingly have come sooner, but I had no power to do so, till this little heathen (pointing to the newborn babe) was come to the light. Now I have free access. Only, fetch no priest from the mainland to christen it, or I must depart again. If you will in this matter comply with my wishes, you may not only continue to live here, but all the good that ever you can wish for I will cause you. Whatever you take in hand shall prosper. Good luck shall follow you wherever you go; but break this condition, and depend upon it that misfortune after misfortune will come on you, and even on this child will I avenge myself. If you want anything, or are in danger, you have only to pronounce my name three times, and I will appear and lend you assistance. I am of the race of the old giants, and my name is Guru. But beware of uttering in my presence the name of him whom no giant may hear of, and never venture to make the sign of the cross, or to cut it on beam or on board of the house. You may dwell in this house the whole year long, only be so good as to give it up to me on Yule evening, when the sun is at the lowest, as then we celebrate our great festival, and then only are we permitted to be merry. At least, if you should not be willing to go out of the house, keep yourselves up in the loft as quiet as possible the whole day long, and, as you value your lives, do not look down into the room until midnight is past. After that you may take possession of everything again.'

When the old woman had thus spoken she vanished, and Aslog and Orm, now at ease respecting their situation, lived, without any disturbance, content and happy. Orm never made a cast of his net without getting a plentiful draught. He never shot an arrow from his bow that missed its aim. In short, whatever they took in hand, were it ever so trifling, evidently prospered.

When Christmas came, they cleaned up the house in the best manner, set everything in order, kindled a fire on the hearth, and, as the twilight approached, they went up to the loft, where they remained quiet and still. At length it grew dark. They thought they heard a sound of flying and labouring in the air, such as the swans make in the wintertime. There was a hole in the roof over the fireplace which might be opened or shut either to let in the light from above or to afford a free passage for the smoke. Orm lifted up the lid, which was covered with a skin, and put out his head, but what a wonderful sight then presented itself to his eyes! The little islands around were all lit up with countless blue lights, which moved about without ceasing, jumped up and down, then skipped down to the shore, assembled together, and now came nearer and nearer to the large island where Orm and Aslog lived. At last they reached it and arranged themselves in a circle around a large stone not far from the shore, and which Orm well knew. What was his surprise when he saw that the stone had now completely assumed the form of a man, though of a monstrous and gigantic one! He could clearly perceive that the little blue lights were borne by dwarfs, whose pale clay-coloured faces, with their huge noses and red eyes, disfigured, too, by birds' bills and owls' eyes, were supported by misshapen bodies. They tottered and wobbled about here and there, so that they seemed to be, at the same time, merry and in pain. Suddenly the circle opened, the little ones retired on each side, and Guru, who was now much enlarged and of as immense a size as the stone, advanced with gigantic steps. She threw both her arms about the stone image, which immediately began to receive life and motion. As soon as the first sign of motion showed itself the little ones began, with wonderful capers and grimaces, a song, or, to speak more properly, a howl, with which the whole island resounded and seemed to tremble. Orm, quite terrified, drew in his head, and he and Aslog remained in the dark, so still that they hardly ventured to draw their breath.

The procession moved on towards the house, as might be clearly perceived by the nearer approach of the shouting and crying. They were now all come in, and, light and active, the dwarfs jumped about on the benches, and heavy and loud sounded, at intervals, the steps of the giants. Orm and his wife heard them covering the table, and the clattering of the plates, and the shouts of joy with which they celebrated their banquet. When it was over, and it drew near to midnight, they began to dance to that ravishing fairy air which charms the mind into such sweet confusion, and which some have heard in the rocky glens, and learned by listening to the underground musicians. As soon as Aslog caught the sound of the air she felt an irresistible longing to see the dance, nor was Orm able to keep her back.

'Let me look,' said she, 'or my heart will burst.'

She took her child and placed herself at the extreme end of the loft whence, without being observed, she could see all that passed. Long did she gaze, without taking off her eyes for an instant, on the dance, on the bold and wonderful springs of the little creatures who seemed to float in the air and not so much as to touch the ground, while the ravishing melody of the elves filled her whole soul. The child, meanwhile, which lay in her arms, grew sleepy and drew its breath heavily, and without ever thinking of the promise she had given to the old woman, she made, as is usual, the sign of the cross over the mouth of the child, and said, 'Christ bless you, my babe!'

The instant she had spoken the word there was raised a horrible, piercing cry. The spirits tumbled head over heels out at the door, with terrible crushing and crowding, their lights went out, and in a few minutes the whole house was clear of them and left desolate. Orm and Aslog, frightened to death, hid themselves in the most retired nook in the house. They did not venture to stir till daybreak, and not till the sun shone through the hole in the roof down on the fireplace did they feel courage enough to descend from the loft.

The table remained still covered as the underground people had left it. All their vessels, which were of silver, and manufactured in the most beautiful manner, were upon it. In the middle of the room there stood upon the ground a huge copper kettle half-full of sweet mead, and, by the side of it, a drinking-horn of pure gold. In the corner lay against the wall a stringed instrument not unlike a dulcimer, which, as people believe, the giantesses used to play on. They gazed on what was before them full of admiration, but without venturing to lay their hands on anything; but great and fearful was their amazement when, on turning about, they saw sitting at the table an immense figure, which Orm instantly recognised as the giant whom Guru had animated by her embrace. He was now a cold and hard stone. While they were standing gazing on it, Guru herself entered the room in her giant form. She wept so bitterly that the tears trickled down on the ground. It was long ere her sobbing permitted her to utter a single word. At length she spoke, 'Great affliction have you brought on me, and henceforth must I weep while I live. I know you have not done this with evil intentions, and therefore I forgive you, though it were a trifle for me to crush the whole house like an eggshell over your heads.'

'Alas!' cried she, 'my husband, whom I love more than myself, there he sits petrified forever. Never again will he open his eyes! Three hundred years lived I with my father on the island of Kunnan, happy in the innocence of youth, as the fairest among the giant maidens. Mighty heroes sued for my hand. The sea around that island is still filled with the rocky fragments which they hurled against each other in their combats. Andfind won the victory, and I plighted myself to him; but ere I was married came the detestable Odin into the country, who overcame my father, and drove us all from the island. My father and sisters fled to the mountains, and since that time my eyes have beheld them no more. Andfind and I saved ourselves on this island, where we for a long time lived in peace and quiet, and thought it would never be interrupted. Destiny, which no one escapes, had determined it otherwise. Oluf came from Britain. They called him the Holy, and Andfind instantly found that his voyage would be inauspicious to the giants. When he heard how Oluf's ship rushed through the waves, he went down to the strand and blew the sea against him with all his strength. The waves swelled up like mountains, but Oluf was still more mighty than he. His ship flew unchecked through the billows like an arrow from a bow. He steered direct for our island. When the ship was so near that Andfind thought he could reach it with his hands, he grasped at the fore-part with his right hand, and was about to drag it down to the bottom, as he had often done with other ships. Then Oluf, the terrible Oluf, stepped forward, and, crossing his hands over each other, he cried with a loud voice, 'Stand there as a stone till the last day!' and in the same instant my unhappy husband became a mass of rock. The ship went on unimpeded, and ran direct against the mountain, which it cut through, separating from it the little island which lies yonder.'

'Ever since my happiness has been annihilated, and lonely and melancholy have I passed my life. On Yule eve alone can petrified giants receive back their life, for the space of seven hours, if one of their race embraces them, and is, at the same time, willing to sacrifice a hundred years of his own life. Seldom does a giant do that. I loved my husband too well not to bring him back cheerfully to life, every time that I could do it, even at the highest price, and never would I reckon how often I had done it that I might not know when the time came when I myself should share his fate, and, at the moment I threw my arms around him, become the same as he. Alas, now even this comfort is taken from me. I can never more by any embrace awake him, since he has heard the name which I dare not utter, and never again will he see the light till the dawn of the last day shall bring it.'

'Now I go hence! You will never again behold me! All that is here in the house I give you! My dulcimer alone will I keep. Let no one venture to fix his habitation on the little islands which lie around here. There dwell the little underground ones whom you saw at the festival, and I will protect them as long as I live.'

With these words Guru vanished. The next spring Orm took the golden horn and the silverware to Trondheim where no one knew him. The value of the things was so great that he was able to purchase everything a wealthy man desires. He loaded his ship with his purchases, and returned to the island, where he spent many years in unalloyed happiness, and Aslog's father was soon reconciled to his wealthy son-in-law.

The stone image remained sitting in the house. No human power was able to move it. So hard was the stone that hammer and axe flew in pieces without making the slightest impression upon it. The giant sat there till a holy man came to the island, who, with one single word, removed him back to his former station, where he stands to this hour. The copper kettle, which the underground people left behind them, was preserved as a memorial upon the island, which bears the name of House Island to the present day.

THE MAGIC PIPE

BY KATHARINE PYLE

There were once three brothers, all the sons of the same father and mother.

The two elder were hard-working, thrifty lads, who had no care except as to how they might better themselves in the world. But the youngest, whose name was Boots, was not thrifty at all. He was a do-nothing and was quite content to sit in the chimney corner and warm his shins and think about things.

One day the eldest son came to his father and said, 'I have it in mind to go over yonder to the king's castle and take service there, for I hear the king has need of a herdsman to take care of his hares for him. The wages are six dollars a week, and if anyone can keep the herd together and bring them safe home every night without losing one of them, the king will give him the princess for a wife.'

The father was pleased when he heard this. Six dollars a week was fair pay, and it would be a fine thing if the lad could win the princess for his wife. At any rate it was worth trying for.

So the eldest son cocked his hat over one ear, and off he set for the palace.

He had not gone so very far when he came to the edge of a forest, and there was an old crone with a green nose a yard long, and it was caught in a crack of a log. She was dancing and hopping about, but for all her dancing and hopping she got no farther than that one spot, for her nose held her there.

The lad stopped and stared at her, and she looked so funny to his mind that he laughed and laughed till his sides ached.

'You gawk!' screamed the old hag. 'Come and drive a wedge in the crack so I can get my nose out. Here I have stood for twice a hundred years, and no Christian soul has come to set me free.'

'If you have stood there twice a hundred years you might as well stay a while longer. As for me, I'm expected at the King's palace, and I have no time to waste driving wedges,' said the lad, and away he went, one foot before the other, leaving the old crone with her nose still in the crack.

When the lad came to the palace, he knocked at the door and told the man who opened it that he had come to see about the place of herdsman. When the man heard this he brought the lad straight to the king, and told him what the lad had come for.

The king listened and nodded his head. Yes, he was in need of a herdsman and would be glad to take the lad into his service, and the wages were just as the youth thought, with a chance of winning the princess to boot. But there was one part of the bargain that had been left out. If the lad failed to keep the herd together and lost so much as even one small leveret, he was to receive such a beating as would turn him black and blue.

That part of the bargain was not such pleasant hearing as the rest of it. Still the lad had a mind to try for the princess. So he was taken out to the paddock where the hares were, and a pretty sight it was to see them hopping and frisking about, hundreds and hundreds of them, big and little.

All morning the hares were kept there in the paddock with the new herdsman watching them, and as long as that was the case everything went well. But later on the hares had to be driven out on the hills for a run and a bite of fresh grass, and then the trouble began. The lad could no more keep them together than if they had been sparks from a fire. Away they sped, someone way and some another, into the woods and over the hills – there was no keeping track of them. The lad shouted and ran, and ran and shouted, till the sweat poured down his face, but he could not herd them back. By the time evening came he had scarce a score of them to drive home to the palace.

And there on the steps stood the king with a stout rod in his hands, all ready to give the lad a beating. And a good beating it was, I can tell you. When the king had finished with him he could hardly stand. Home he went with only his sore bones for wages.

Then it was the second brother's turn. He also had a mind to try his hand at keeping the king's hares, with the chance of winning the princess for a wife. Off he set along the same road his brother had taken, and after a while he came to the place where the old crone was dancing about with her long green nose still caught in the crack of a log. He was just as fond of a good laugh as his brother was, and he stood for a while to watch her, for he thought it a merry sight. He laughed and laughed till the tears ran down his cheeks, and the old hag was screaming with rage.

'You gawk! Come and drive a wedge into the crack so that I can get my nose out,' she bawled. 'Here I have been for twice a hundred years and no Christian soul has come to set me free.'

'If you have been there that long it will not hurt to stay a bit longer,' said the youth. 'I'm no woodsman, and besides that I'm on my way to the king's palace to win a princess for a wife.' And away he went, leaving the old woman screaming after him.

After a while the second brother came to the palace, and when the servants heard why he had come they were not slow in bringing him before the king. Yes, the king was as much in need of a herdsman for his hares as ever, but was the lad willing to run the risk of having only a beating for his pains?

Yes, the lad was willing to run that risk, for he was almost sure he could keep the herd together, and it was not every day one had a chance of winning a princess for a wife.

So they took him out to the paddock where the hares were. All morning he herded them there as his brother had done before him, and that was an easy task. But it was in the afternoon that the trouble began. For no sooner did the fresh wind of the hillside ruffle up their fur than away they fled, this way and that, kicking up their heels behind them. It was in vain the lad chased after them and shouted and sweated; he could not keep them together. In the end he had scarcely threescore of them to drive back to the palace in the evening.

And the king was waiting for him with a cudgel in his hands, and if the lad did not get a good drubbing that day, then nobody ever did. When the king finished with him he was black and blue from his head to his heels, and that is all he got for trying to win a princess for a wife.

Now after the second son had come home again with his doleful tale, Boots sat and thought and thought about what had happened. After a while, however, he rose up and shook the ashes from his clothes and said that now it was his turn to have a try at winning the princess for his wife.

When the elder brothers heard that they scoffed and hooted. Boots was no better than a numskull anyway, and how could he hope to succeed where they had failed.

Well, all that might be true or it might not, but at any rate he was for having a try at this business, so off he set, just as the other two had before him.

After a while he came to the log where his brothers had seen the hag with her nose caught in the crack, and there she was still, for no one had come by in the meantime to set her free. He stood and stared and stared, for it was a curious sight.

'Oh, you gawk! Why do you stand there staring?' cried the old hag. 'Here I have been for twice a hundred years, and no Christian soul will take the trouble to set me free. Drive a wedge into the crack so that I may get my nose out.'

'That I will and gladly, good mother,' said the youth. 'Two hundred years is a long time for one to have one's nose pinched in a crack.'

Quickly he found a wedge and drove it into the crack with a stone, and then the old hag pulled her nose out.

'Now you have done me a good turn, and I have it in mind to do the same for you,' she said. With that she took a pretty little pipe out of the pocket of her skirt. 'Do you take this,' she said, 'and it will come in handy if you're on your way to the King's palace. If you blow on the right end of the whistle the things around you will be blown every which way as if a strong wind had struck them, and if you blow on the wrong end of it they will be gathered together again. And those are not the only tricks the pipe has, for if anyone takes it from you, you have only to wish for it, and you can wish it back into your fingers again.'

Boots took the pipe and thanked the old hag kindly, and then he bade her goodbye and went on his way to the king's palace.

When the king heard what Boots had come for, he was no less ready to take him for a herdsman than he had been to take his brothers. 'But, mind you, you shall have a drubbing that will make your bones ache if you come back in the evening with even the smallest leveret missing from the herd,' said the king.

Yes, that was all right, the lad was ready to take the risk. So all morning Boots herded the hares in the paddock, and in the afternoon he took them out to the hills, as the bargain was. There the hares could no longer be kept in a herd. They kicked up their heels and away they went, every which way.

So that was the game, was it? Boots was very willing to play it, too. He took out his pipe and blew a tune on the right end of it, and away the hares flew faster than they had intended, as though a strong wind had blown them. Presently there was not one left on the hill. Then the lad lay down in the sun and fell asleep.

When he awoke it was toward evening and time to be bringing the hares back to the castle, but not one of them was in sight.

Then Boots sat up, and shook the hair out of his eyes and blew on the wrong end of the pipe. Immediately there was the whole herd before him, drawn up in ranks just like soldiers. Not even one of the smallest leverets was missing.

'That is well,' said Boots. 'And now we'll be going home again.'

Off he set for the palace, driving the hares before him, and as soon as he came near enough he could see the king standing on the steps waiting for him with a stout cudgel in his hand, for he had no thought but that Boots would fail in his task.

When he saw the whole herd come hopping home, as tame as sheep, and turning into the paddock, he could hardly believe his eyes. He hurried after and began to count them. He counted them over and over again, and not one was missing.

Well, Boots had brought them all back safely that time, but the question was whether he could do it again.

Boots thought he could. Indeed, he was sure he could. So the next afternoon he set out for the hills, whistling merrily as he tramped along with the hares hopping before him.

That day things happened just as they had before. As soon as the hares began to stray Boots took his pipe and blew them away as though they were so much chaff. He lay down and slept until it was time to take them home again, and then he blew them together with the wrong end of the pipe.

When the king found the lad had brought the whole herd home again for the second time he was greatly troubled, for he had no mind to give the princess to Boots for a bride. So the third day he bade the princess go out to the hills and hide herself among the bushes and watch and see how it was that Boots managed to keep the hares together.

This the princess did. She hid behind the bushes; she saw Boots come tramping up the hill with the hares frisking before him; she saw him blow them away with his pipe as though they had been so many dry leaves in the wind, and then, after he had had a nap, she saw him blow them together again.

Then the princess must and would have that pipe. She came out from the bushes and offered to buy it. She offered ten dollars for it.

'No.'

'Fifty!'

'No!'

'A hundred!'

'No.' Boots had no wish to sell, but as it was the princess, and as she seemed so set and determined on having it, he would tell her what he would do; he would sell the pipe for a hundred dollars if she would give him a kiss for every dollar she paid.

The princess did not know what to say to that. It was not becoming that a princess should kiss a herdsman; still she wanted the pipe and as that was the only way to get it she at last agreed. She paid the lad a hundred bright silver dollars, and she also gave him a hundred kisses out there on the hillside, with no one to look on but the hares.

Then she took the pipe and hastened home with it.

But small good the pipe did her. Just as she reached the palace steps the pipe slipped out of her fingers as though it had been buttered, and look as she might she could not find it again.

That was because the lad had wished it back to himself. At that very moment he was on his way home with the pipe in his pocket and the hares hopping before him in lines like soldiers.

When the king heard the story he thought and pondered. The princess had told him nothing of the kisses. He thought she had bought the pipe for a hundred dollars, so the next day he sent the queen out to the hillside with two hundred dollars in her pocket.

'The princess is young and foolish,' said he. 'She must have lost the pipe on the hillside, and no doubt the lad has it back by this time. Do you go out and see if you can buy it from him and if you once have your fingers on it you'll not lose it, I'll wager.'

So the queen went out to the hillside and hid herself in the bushes, and she saw Boots blow the hares away and lie down to sleep and afterward blow them together again in a twinkling.

Then she came out from the bushes and offered to buy the pipe. At first the lad said no, and again no, and then no for the third time, but in the end he sold the pipe to the queen for two hundred dollars and fifty kisses to go with them, and the queen hoped the king would never hear of it. She took the pipe and hastened home with it, but she fared no better than the princess, for just before she reached the palace the pipe disappeared from her fingers, and what had become of it she did not know.

When the King heard that he was a wroth and angry man. Now he himself would go out to the hill and buy the pipe, for there was no trusting the womenfolk. If he once had the pipe in his hands there would be no losing it again, and of that he felt very sure. So he mounted his old mare, Whitey, and rode over to the hillside. There he hid himself among the bushes, and he hid old Whitey there with him, and he watched until he had seen all that the others had told him about. Then he came out and tried to strike a bargain with the lad. But this time it seemed as though Boots would not sell the pipe – neither for love nor money. The king offered him three hundred dollars, and four hundred dollars, and five hundred dollars for it, and still Boots said no.

'Listen!' said Boots suddenly. 'If you'll go over there in the bushes and kiss old Whitey on the mouth five-and-twenty times, I'll sell you the pipe for five hundred dollars, but not otherwise.'

That was a thing the king was loath to do, for it ill befitted a king to kiss an old horse, but have the pipe he must and would; and besides there was nobody there to see him do it but Boots, and he did not count. 'May I spread a handkerchief between old Whitey's mouth and mine before I do it?' asked the king.

Yes, he might do that.

So the king went back into the bushes and spread his handkerchief over old Whitey's mouth and kissed her through it five-and-twenty times. Then he came back and the lad gave him the pipe, and the king mounted and rode away with it, and he was well pleased with himself for his cleverness, and he held the pipe tight in one hand and the bridle in the other. 'No danger of my losing it as the queen and the princess did,' thought he. But scarcely had the king reached the palace steps when the pipe slipped through his fingers like water, and what became of it he did not know.

But when Boots drove the hares home that evening he had the pipe safely hidden away up his sleeve, though nobody knew it.

And now how about the princess? Would the king keep his promise and give her to the herdsman for a wife?

But that was a thing the king and queen could not bear to think of.

They put their heads together and talked and talked, and the more they talked the more unwilling they were to have a herdsman in the family. So in the end this is what they said. The princess was a very clever girl, and she must have a clever lad for a husband. If Boots could tell bigger stories than the princess then he should have her for a wife, but if she could tell bigger stories than he, then he should have three red strips cut from his back and be beaten all the way home.

To this Boots agreed.

Then the princess began. 'I looked out of my window,' said she, 'and there was a tree that grew straight up to the sky, and the fruit of it was diamonds and pearls and rubies. I reached out and picked them and made myself such a necklace as never was, and I might have it yet only I leaned over the well to look at myself in the waters, and the necklace fell off, and there it lies still at the bottom of the well for anyone who cares to dive for it.'

'That is a pretty story!' said Boots, 'but I can tell a better. When I was herding hares the princess came up on the hill and gave me a hundred bright silver dollars and a hundred kisses as well, one for every dollar.'

Then the king scowled till his brows met, and the princess grew as red as fire. 'Oh, what a story!' cried she.

Then it was her turn again.

'I went to see my godmother, and she took me for a ride in a golden coach drawn by six fleas, and the fleas were as big as horses, and they went so fast we were back again a day before we started.'

'That's a good story,' said Boots, 'but here's a better. The queen came out on the hillside and made me a present of two hundred dollars, and she kissed me over and over again; fifty kisses she gave me.'

'Is that true?' said the king to the queen, and his face was as black as thunder.

'It's a great wicked story,' cried the queen, 'and you must know it is.'

Then the princess tried again. 'I had six suitors, and I cared for one no more than another, but the seventh one was a demon, and he would have had me whether or no. He would have flown away with me before this, but I caught his tail in the crack of the door, and he howled most horribly. There he is still, if you care to look, unless he has vanished in a puff of smoke.'

'Now it is my turn,' said Boots, 'and you may believe this or not, but it's mostly true. The king came up on the hillside and kissed the old white mare twenty-five times. I was there and I saw. He kissed her twenty-five times, and he gave me five hundred dollars not to tell.'

When Boots told this right out before everyone, the king was so ashamed he did not know which way to look. 'There's not a word of it true. It's the biggest story I ever heard,' said he.

'Very well, then I have won the princess,' said Boots. 'And when shall we be married?'

And married they were that day week, for the king and queen could no longer refuse to give Boots the princess for a wife.

The princess was willing, too, for Boots was a handsome, fine-looking lad. They had a great feast at the wedding, with plenty of cake and ale flowing like water. I was there, and I ate and drank with the best of them.

Pfst! There goes a mouse. Catch it and you may make a fine big cloak of its skin – and that's a story, too.

THE GREAT WHITE BEAR AND THE TROLLS

BY KATHARINE PYLE

There was once a man in Finmark named Halvor, who had a great white bear, and this great white bear knew many tricks. One day the man thought to himself, 'This bear is very wonderful. I will take it as a present to the King of Denmark, and perhaps he will give me in return a whole bag of money.' So he set out along the road to Denmark, leading the bear behind him.

He journeyed on and journeyed on, and after a while he came to a deep, dark forest. There was no house in sight, and as it was almost night Halvor began to be afraid he would have to sleep on the ground, with only the trees overhead for a shelter.

Presently, however, he heard the sound of a woodcutter's axe. He followed the sound, and soon he came to an opening in the forest. There, sure enough, was a man hard at work cutting down trees. 'And wherever there's a man,' thought Halvor to himself, 'there must be a house for him to live in.'

'Good day,' said Halvor.

'Good day!' answered the man, staring with all his eyes at the great white bear.

'Will you give us shelter for the night, my bear and me?' asked Halvor. 'And will you give us a bit of food too? I will pay you well if you will.'

'Gladly would I give you both food and shelter,' answered the man, 'but tonight, of all nights in the year, no one may stop in my home except at the risk of his life.'

'How is that?' asked Halvor; and he was very much surprised.

'Why, it is this way. This is the eve of St John, and on every St John's Eve all the trolls in the forest come to my house. I am obliged to spread a feast for them, and there they stay all night, eating and drinking. If they found anyone in the house at that time, they would surely tear him to pieces. Even I and my wife dare not stay. We are obliged to spend the night in the forest.'

'This is a strange business,' said Halvor. 'Nevertheless, I have a mind to stop there and see what these same trolls look like. As to their hurting me, as long as I have my bear with me there is nothing in the world that I am afraid of.'

The woodcutter was alarmed at these words. 'No, no; do not risk it, I beg of you!' he cried. 'Do you spend the night with us out under the trees, and tomorrow we can safely return to our home.'

But Halvor would not listen to this. He was determined to sleep in a house that night, and, moreover, he had a great curiosity to see what trolls looked like.

'Very well,' said the woodcutter at last, 'since you are determined to risk your life, do you follow yonder path, and it will soon bring you to my house.'

Halvor thanked him and went on his way, and it was not long before he and his bear reached the woodcutter's home. He opened the door and went in, and when he saw the feast the woodcutter had spread for the trolls his mouth fairly watered to taste of it. There were sausages and ale and fish and cakes and rice porridge and all sorts of good things. He tasted a bit here and there and gave his bear some, and then he sat down to wait for the coming of the trolls. As for the bear, he lay down beside his master and went to sleep.

They had not been there long when a great noise arose in the forest outside. It was a sound of moaning and groaning and whistling and shrieking. So loud and terrible it grew that Halvor was frightened in spite of himself. The cold crept up and down his back and the hair rose on his head. The sound came nearer and nearer, and by the time it reached the door Halvor was so frightened that he could bear it no longer. He jumped up and ran to the stove. Quickly he opened the oven door and hid himself inside, pulling the door to behind him. The great white bear paid no attention, however, but only snored in his sleep.

Scarcely was Halvor inside the oven when the door of the house was burst open and all the trolls of the forest came pouring into the room.

There were big trolls and little trolls, fat trolls and thin. Some had long tails and some had short tails and some had no tails at all. Some had two eyes and some had three, and some had only one set in the middle of the forehead. One there was, and the others called him Long Nose, who had a nose as long and as thin as a poker.

The trolls banged the door behind them, and then they gathered round the table where the feast was spread.

'What is this?' cried the biggest troll in a terrible voice (and Halvor's heart trembled within him). 'Someone has been here before us. The food has been tasted and ale has been spilled.'

At once Long Nose began snuffing about. 'Whoever has been here is here still,' he cried. 'Let us find him and tear him to pieces.'

'Here is his pussycat, anyway,' cried the smallest troll of all, pointing to the white bear. 'Oh, what a pretty cat it is! Pussy! Pussy! Pussy!' And the little troll put a piece of sausage on a fork and stuck it against the white bear's nose.

At that the great white bear gave a roar and rose to its feet. It gave the troll a blow with its paw that sent him spinning across the room. He of the long nose had it almost broken off, and the big troll's ears rang with the box he got. This way and that the trolls were knocked and beaten by the bear, until at last they tore the door open and fled away into the forest, howling.

When they had all gone Halvor crawled out and closed the door, and then he and the white bear sat down and feasted to their hearts' content. After that the two of them lay down and slept quietly for the rest of the night.

In the morning the woodcutter and his family stole back to the house and peeped in at the window. What was their surprise to see Halvor and his bear sitting there and eating their breakfasts as though nothing in the world had happened to them.

'How is this?' cried the woodcutter. 'Did the trolls not come?'

'Oh, yes, they came,' answered Halvor, 'but we drove them away, and I do not think they will trouble you again.' He then told the woodcutter all that had happened in the night. 'After the beating they received, they will be in no hurry to visit you again,' he said.

The woodcutter was filled with joy and gratitude when he heard this. He and his wife entreated Halvor to stay there in the forest and make his home with them, but this he refused to do. He was on his way to Denmark to sell his bear to the king, and to Denmark he would go. So off he set, after saying goodbye, and the good wishes of the woodcutter and his wife went with him.

Now the very next year, on St John's Eve, the woodcutter was out in the forest cutting wood, when a great ugly troll stuck his head out of a tree near by.

'Woodcutter! Woodcutter!' he cried.

'Well,' said the woodcutter, 'what is it?'

'Tell me, have you that great white cat with you still?'

'Yes, I have; and, moreover, now she has five kittens, and each one of them is larger and stronger than she is.'

'Is that so?' cried the troll, in a great fright. 'Then goodbye, woodcutter, for we will never come to your house again.'

Then he drew in his head and the tree closed together, and that was the last the woodcutter heard or saw of the trolls. After that he and his family lived undisturbed and unafraid.

As for Halvor, he had already reached Denmark, and the king had been so pleased with the bear that he paid a whole bag of money for it, just as Halvor had hoped, and with that bag of money Halvor set up in trade so successfully that he became one of the richest men in Denmark.